Seeing Dallas asleep, Cory ached with love for him

She wanted to cross the dim hospital waiting room to the chair where he was slumped and run her fingers through his jet-black hair, trace the proud curve of his high cheekbone with her finger, and cradle his head against her shoulder.

"I've been forced to do some things I would rather not have done," he'd told her quietly. What had he meant? What could have forced him? Necessity and hunger? And what would he have done?

Where have you been, Dallas, she questioned the sleeping face. *What have you done to make you the man you are? And why won't you let me in? Why won't you ever let me get close to you?*

Quinn Wilder is a Canadian writer, born and raised in Calgary, who now lives in the Okanagan Valley away from the bustle of a city. She has had a variety of jobs, but her favorite pastime has always been writing. She graduated from the Southern Alberta Institute of Technology Journalism Arts program in 1979. Since then she has free-lanced, and her list of credits includes magazine articles, educational material, scripts and speeches. Her first novel became a Harlequin, marking a high point in her career. She enjoys skiing and horseback riding.

That Man from Texas

Quinn Wilder

Harlequin Books

TORONTO • NEW YORK • LONDON
AMSTERDAM • PARIS • SYDNEY • HAMBURG
STOCKHOLM • ATHENS • TOKYO • MILAN

Original hardcover edition published in 1985
by Mills & Boon Limited

ISBN 0-373-02772-9

Harlequin Romance first edition June 1986

Printed in U.S.A.

CHAPTER ONE

CORY MCCONNEL sighed, hooked her cowboy boot clad foot in the lowest rung of the fence, and rested her head on her arms. Where was Dad? she wondered for at least the fortieth time, focusing her attention on the main gravel road and searching for that tell tale cloud of dust that would signal a vehicle coming. There was none, and Cory's attention drifted lazily to the cattle in the field she was overlooking. Two calves romped playfully, oblivious to the havoc their sharp little hooves were inflicting on the delicate blue-violet blooms of the wild crocuses. Cory found herself smiling at their antics despite the anxiousness growing in the pit of her stomach.

Her smile disappeared as the May breeze stirred the sign at the end of her own long gravel drive into a gentle swing. She couldn't read the sign from her post at the fence, but then she didn't have to read it. Its message was committed to memory.

For Sale. Just like that. A cold 'for sale', followed by an impersonal description of the property in question. The sign, Cory thought resentfully, failed to mention what was really for sale—a family's entire history, her own laughter-filled childhood memories, and even the small neatly kept grave where her mother was buried. It seemed to Cory like her entire life was up for sale with this ranch.

Her eyes, dark and velvety brown, grew darker as she recalled the night that Dad had called her into the tiny and disarrayed room that he proudly referred to as his den.

'I'm going to sell the ranch, Cory.' In dazed disbelief she had listened as he told her how, for the past five years, profits had been dwindling. This year, he had confided sadly and with some bewilderment, they would be operating in the red.

'It's this dang economy thing, Cor. I can't fight it anymore. And I'm too old to know how to turn things around. And there's you to think about, too. Did you know that Nancy Jacobsen just got back from six months in Europe? Gad, Cory, that's the type of experience you deserve! You should be going to Europe, or to university; doing what other kids your age are doing—not hanging around this ranch doing double duty as a hand. I've always had a hankering to see Europe myself. If we sold, Cor, you and me could go together, and really see Europe in style.'

'I don't want to go to Europe,' Cory had wailed. 'And I don't want to go to university. Everything I want, and will ever want, is right here on the Flying M.' She searched her mind desperately for a solution. 'Dad, we can sell some of it to the munchies—that would keep us going, get us through.'

Her father had stared at her in horror. The 'munchies' was Cory and Mac McConnel's pet name for the people who were gobbling up farm and range land in the magnificent Canadian Rocky Mountain foothills for acreages.

'I couldn't sell my land to the munchies, Cor,' he'd said slowly, obviously pained that his own flesh and blood could contemplate such a crime. 'My Daddy homesteaded this land. He saw it for what it was—the finest ranch land in the world. He built it with his own hands, and if I must lose it, I'll lose it as a whole, and I'll lose it knowing that it's still going to be ranched. I'd die before I'd let one acre of it be used for some high-falutin' house and a swimming pool.'

When had he got so old? Cory had wondered at that moment. Without her really noticing, his hair had gone from salt and pepper to pure white, the once broad shoulders had a slight stoop to them, and slender had become thin. On his next birthday she realised with a start, he would be sixty-five.

He loved the Flying M she realised painfully, just as much as she did. It wasn't just his home but also his profession. It was his whole life and he'd built that life not just with his hands, but also with his heart.

She wished with sudden tenderness that he could have shared the burden of the last five years with her. Instead, he had probably spent many an evening in this little den, lonely and afraid, and struggling desperately to keep his ranch. He wouldn't have shared that with her, she knew, because he wouldn't have wanted her to worry. Despite her eighteen years, she was still his little girl, and he still took his role as protector and provider as seriously as he had when she was six.

She thought, guiltily, of the carefree lifestyle she'd enjoyed since graduating from high school nearly a year ago. She'd wanted, of course to get a job, but Mac had been adamant in his refusal to even discuss the matter, never once letting on that the ranch was experiencing financial difficulties.

He had insisted she take a year or two to do just what she wanted—hinting he would have been extremely pleased if 'just what she wanted' was to go to Europe or university. He had a fixed and old-fashioned idea that these were proper pursuits for a young lady—whereas working definitely was not. He was a proud man, and would have indulged her every whim without ever letting on they couldn't afford it.

For a year Cory had dutifully been sending for university prospectuses which she never looked at, but left lying around the house until she was sure Mac had seen them. She had no illusions about being university material. She hated being inside and had been heartily relieved when she'd managed to graduate with average grades. She also hated the implication that the campus was a happy hunting ground for a man to marry.

Mac was as adamant she wasn't going to work around the ranch as he had been that she wasn't going to work anywhere else, but after a few months of having her at home, his vigilance had slowly eroded. Mostly he turned a blind eye to the jobs she was taking on around the ranch, though occasionally, grudgingly, he would ask her to run an errand for him.

Basically, she was an errand girl—running into town for a forgotten piece of equipment, mending a fence nobody else had time for, sitting up through the night nursing a sick animal. But what she loved best was working with their young horses. Mac would have died before he would have allowed her to be the one who actually got in the saddle and broke the horse, but she considered the job she did just as essential, and even Mac reluctantly admired her talent with the skittish young animals, while never quite admitting it was work. Cory gentled the animals, sometimes spending a whole day sitting patiently waiting for a nervous foal to come take sugar from her, or rubbing down a high-strung two-year old with a soft chamois cloth. Her own spirited black quarter-horse mare was a testament to her ability with horses, and in the spring and summer they were rarely separated as Cory untiringly explored the unfolding majesty of the foothills of her home.

Questions of who she was, or where life was taking her simply didn't cross her mind. The Flying M kept her busy and content, and she was stunned that her idyllic life was drawing to a close.

She wanted to beg, to throw a tantrum, to weep—anything to make Mac understand that she couldn't live without her ranch. And yet the grey look of stoic despair on his face silenced her protest. She swallowed her selfish concerns.

'Dad,' Cory had said bravely, understanding that she must not make this decision any harder for him than it already was, 'if you say we must sell, then we must sell.' And then she flew into his outstretched arms and they both wept over the fate of their beloved Flying M.

The next day the sign had gone up, and gloom had descended over the ranch. The three ranch hands had been particuarly unhappy. They were in danger of losing not just their 'family', but their jobs, and for two of them, their homes as well.

That had been six months ago, and as it became apparent that the chances of selling such a large holding in such tough times were slim, things slowly returned to normal. Most of the time, Cory didn't even give a thought to the swaying sign at the end of the drive. And Mac seemed to be more delighted than worried that the ranch wasn't attracting many prospects.

A cloud of dust rising above the road brought Cory back to the present. The huge black sedan of the real estate agent came into view over the rise. Despite the news it might be bringing, Cory allowed herself a small smile at the sight of the luxurious car. Dad had told her last night that they had finally had a serious offer.

'And get this, Cor,' he'd said, 'that real estate man's going to drive all the way out here in that fancy car of his, pick me up, and drive me into Calgary, then drive me home again. Can you figure that?' He'd shaken his great mane of white curls in obvious irritation at the wasteful and baffling ways of city folk.

But this morning, Cory had found him sitting on the front steps looking for all the world like a little boy anxious about his first day of school. 'Do I look okay, Cor? I never met a rich business man before.'

Or ridden in a car like that, she'd thought wryly, as she surveyed his appearance. The suit was the same one he'd worn to Mom's funeral twelve years ago. Tilda, the ranch cook and their housekeeper, had managed to make it look quite respectable; an effort Mac had effectively nullified by putting on his worn and barn-yard battered boots with it.

'You look just like a good rancher should, Dad,' Cory had assured him. The car had pulled up, and with a breezy I-do-this-everyday kind of wave Mac McConnel had been off to meet his rich business man, and perhaps Cory had thought with a sinking heart, to sell the Flying M.

Cory held her breath now as the agent's car pulled up in front of the sign. 'Go by it,' she whispered, closing her eyes and childishly crossing her fingers. But when she opened her eyes, the salesman was ceremoniously placing a huge red 'sold' sticker across the width of the sign. He got back in the car and turned into the drive.

Slowly, Cory turned away from her post at the fence and walked across the huge expanse of grass that Mac insisted on calling lawn despite the fact it had never been mowed and was full of knee-high weeds. Don't cry, she told herself fiercely, don't you dare cry, Cory McConnel! She looked studiously away from the rambling white two-storey farmhouse she was approaching. As old and unstylish as it was, it was still the only place she had ever called home. With a huge effort she forced a bright smile on to her lips.

The real estate agent and her father had emerged from the car, and both turned to watch her approaching. Her short brown hair, glowing with red highlights under the June sun, bobbed around the pixie face that was dominated by her large, expressive eyes. Even a bulky plaid shirt, and the straight, boyish line of her jeans, could not hide the soft bloom of womanhood that was adding gentle curves to her slim figure.

'Cory's such a lovely girl,' the agent commented, turning back to Mac. 'She does deserve more than this ranch as a life. She'll love Europe.' He pumped Mac's hand energetically. 'Believe me,' he said, sensing the older man's doubt, 'you've done the right thing.' Uncomfortable with the lack of response, he consulted his watch. 'I have to run.' He gave Cory a wave, revved the powerful car unnecessarily, and headed down the lane, followed by a cloud of dust.

Cory kept her smile fixed, though her face was beginning to feel stiff from the effort. 'So, you sold?' she asked, amazed at how collected she sounded.

Mac studied his daughter's face astutely. Despite the smile, her eyes, soft as a doe deer's, denied her brave attempt to be cheerful.

He nodded, and threw a wiry arm over Cory's slender shoulders. 'What say, Cor, we don't even pretend to be brave? We'll have us a good stiff drink, and a good hard cry, and talk about it.'

'That sounds great,' she admitted, snuggling into his arm, and walking with him up the creaking old steps to the house.

'Tilda,' he bawled as soon as they entered the house, 'me and Cor want a drink—and I don't mean lemonade! Come to think of it, you have one, too.'

Tilda's large round face popped out from behind the kitchen door. 'You're in the house,' she admonished sternly, 'not shouting over a tractor engine. And what's this about drinks at this time of day?'

The rest of her huge figure emerged from behind the kitchen door, and she placed her hands on her solid hips, the twinkle in her Santa Claus eyes belying her stern stance.

Tilda had been looking after the McConnels since Cory's mother had been killed in a farm accident. Cory realised with a start that she and Mac had never discussed what would become of Tilda if the ranch was sold. They should have talked, she thought unhappily, but it was so like Dad to just blissfully put off crossing every bridge until he was right on top of them.

'The ranch is sold, Tilda,' Mac said in a tone that was dangerously close to being gentle.

For a moment Tilda's lip trembled, and her eyes filled with tears that didn't quite spill over. Cory felt a lump rise in her own throat and was thankful when Tilda made an admirable effort to show composure.

'I still have supper to cook,' she told Mac unevenly.

'You never mind supper. Bring us all a drink.' It was the closest Mac had ever come to giving Tilda an order, and unsettled with himself, he marched into the plainly furnished living room without waiting for a reply.

'This guy,' he was telling Cory when Tilda came in with a tray of drinks, 'is more than I could have asked for. He's a young fellow—well, not to you— I guess him to be thirty-five or six, but he's ambitious, and he's already got some ideas for turning the ranch around. He was in complete agreement with the clause that says not one inch of this land can be sold to the munchies. I guess what I'm trying to say, is that he never once struck me as being a rich business man. He's like me—a rancher. Geez, if you've gotta sell a place like the Flying M, it sure feels good to sell it to someone you like.

'And he's going to keep on any of the hands who want to stay. That'll sure be good news for the boys.'

Cory noticed that Tilda wasn't mentioned, and she turned swiftly to her. She felt the lump thicken in her own throat again when she observed the ashen face.

'And the cook?' Tilda asked softly and painfully.

'The cook?' Mac bellowed. 'The cook is going to Europe with me and Cor, of course.'

So, he had thought about it, Cory thought with immense relief. 'That's wonderful!' she exclaimed. The only wonderful thing about the whole deal, she added grimly to herself.

'Me?' Tilda whispered, her blue eyes wide with amazement. 'You want me to go with you?' The tears that had been threatening finally spilled over.

'Now, Tilda, don't go making no big deal out of it,' Mac mumbled gruffly. 'It's just you got Cory and me so spoiled that we'd starve to death if we went anywhere without you. Starve to death and walk around in wrinkly clothes. God knows, this daughter of mine ain't handy with a cooking pot and iron.' As an afterthought he added, 'She's good with horses, though.'

Tilda sighed, and Cory glared at her father for providing an opening for this familiar argument.

Tilda responded on cue. 'It's time Cory learned those things, Mac. Someday a man might want to marry Cory and the way things stand now, he'd find her woefully wanting.'

'The world's changing, Tilda,' Cory insisted, a bit wearily. 'Those things aren't as important as they were when you were growing up.'

'Some things don't change,' Tilda asserted stubbornly. 'A man still wants to come in from a hard day's work to smell something cooking. You have to start thinking about your future, Cory. Your Daddy and I aren't going to be here forever to look after you. Even if, heaven forbid, you turn out to be one of these new-fangled women who doesn't want to get married you've still got to know how to cook for yourself.'

Cory sighed. 'I can open a can of beans, you know.'

Mac snorted, and Cory knew that Tilda had won the argument again. Thankfully, it was an argument that she only won in principle. Though Mac whole-heartedly agreed that Cory should learn some of the rudimentaries of cooking and looking after a house, he was remiss to force her to do anything about it.

'She's just a kid,' he'd say when Tilda approached him on the subject. 'She'll only be young once. Let her do what she wants. 'Sides, nobody will be thinking of marrying my little girl for years yet.'

Somehow Mac had never really noticed that his little girl had grown up. But then it was a fact that Cory barely acknowledged either. Life on the ranch simply didn't require it of her. The other girls in the community were either married, or energetically pursuing all the possibilities. Their attitudes towards men left Cory feeling slightly in disdain of them, or more honestly, slightly baffled by them. She didn't see any attractions to marriage, and saw even fewer to dating.

Cory, though she hadn't considered it, and wouldn't have seen the merit if she had, could have easily been among the most popular girls in the district. She would have been astounded to learn that she was considered attractive, down-to-earth, and fun to be with. And she probably wouldn't have cared.

From her point of view, dating had been disastrous. She could eat dinner at home, she always thought practically, and Tilda's cooking was far better than the fare at the Valley's most popular restaurant. She could get her toes stepped on working with horses, she didn't have to go to a dance. If she wanted to go to a movie, she liked to pick which one it was going to be. And the awkward pawing and wet sticky kisses always seemed like the perfect ending for what Cory inevitably felt had been a dreadful evening and a terrible waste of time.

Timmy Stubbs provided the one exception to Cory's ill feelings about dating, and he provided it only because he was content to leave their relationship at friendship. He was always available when an occasion required a date, or for a ride on a Sunday afternoon. He refrained from whispering silly things in her ear, like how nice her hair smelled. He never tried to impress her by driving too fast, drinking too much, or showing off in front of her. Best of all, he was content with a light good night peck and never tried to involve her in the long and tangled kind of kisses that left her feeling squeamish and disgusted. Cory knew that after a year of seeing only Timmy she was known as his 'girl'. The expression seemed to mean nothing to him, and certainly meant nothing to her, though it did give her the distinct advantage of not having to fend off unwanted suitors.

Cory pulled herself out of thought and listened to Mac.

'We're not gonna be rich,' he was saying happily, 'not with all the bills that have to be paid out, and mortgages and the like, but we're gonna have us some money; more money than I ever had before! We'll go to Europe, and when we get back we'll have enough to buy a little place outright. Hell, it won't be the Flying M, but it'll be big enough to run a few head on, and raise a few chickens.'

Cory found herself drifting again. Europe. Somehow she couldn't get excited about the prospect. She let her gaze drift out the window. What could be more impressive than this? she wondered. The sun was setting and the sky was stretching for miles in rainbow tones of pink and orange and purple. The mountains in the distance were black, like cut-outs, against the bright sky.

The foothills held all the marvels that Cory felt she would ever want to see—laughing little brooks and cascading waterfalls; deer that looked at her with huge curious eyes when she happened into their clearings. She sighed and supposed she wasn't very sophisticated for being so content with where she was, and so terrifically unenthused about going to Europe.

'The men will be in for supper soon,' Tilda observed, following Cory's gaze to the quickly darkening sky. 'I better go.'

Mac, determined not to lose the one member of his audience who had been paying any attention to him, wandered out after her still talking.

Cory turned again to the window. She could hear the men now, and make out the shadowy outlines by the corrals. The horses were stomping impatiently to be rid of their saddles, and the crickets were beginning their night songs. In the distance she could hear the lowing of cattle. The sounds were so familiar and comforting and Cory felt a terrible stab of loss when she tried to envision life without these sounds—without all the little things that made the Flying M such a special place to call home.

She got up slowly to go wash for supper. At least the possession date was a couple months away, Cory thought looking determinedly for a bright spot. At least she would have time to say a proper goodbye.

The hands were in when she came back downstairs and she regarded them affectionately. Dutch and Cameron, like Tilda, were people that Cory thought of as members of her own family. Dutch was as old, or perhaps even older than her father, and for all his gruff exterior he was as gentle and kind a man as Cory had ever known.

Cameron was like a brother. Married just recently, and in his early twenties, Cameron and Cory loved to tease each other, and a fond camaraderie existed between them. She felt another wrench of deep loss as she looked at these two—her friends and her family.

Shorty, the foreman, hadn't been a part of the ranch for as long as either Dutch or Cameron. The line between employee and 'family' remained in place where he was concerned, at least for Cory. Though she respected his skills, and though he had always been pleasant to her, she had once seen him lose his temper with a horse, and the vividness with which she recalled that ugly scene always made her vaguely wary of him.

'Well,' Mac announced after the last spoonful of chocolate pudding had disappeared down Cameron's throat, 'sold the ranch.'

The silence was awful and Cory could have shot him for, characteristically, holding the moment to its full dramatic potential. Cameron, especially, looked sick.

'The new owner wants to keep you all on.'

Cameron let out a whoop, and then caught himself, and looked around shamefaced. 'Sorry, I didn't mean I wouldn't miss you and Cory. Just,' a grin spread over his homely freckled face, 'I'm going to be a family man pretty soon, and I didn't know what else a dumb old cowpoke like me could do for a living.'

'That's for sure,' Cory teased, ducking expertly from the spoon he tossed lightly at her.

Later that night, she lay awake thinking about Cameron and Dutch. She hoped desperately they would be happy. But what if the new owner was impossible to work for? What if he didn't understand that Dutch was getting old and couldn't do all the things a younger man might be able to do? What if he didn't understand how hard Cameron had worked to be able to take some time off when his and Shelly's baby was born?

Still puzzling over the problems of her own tiny world, she finally fell asleep to the soft crooning of the crickets, and the faraway and lonesome cry of a coyote.

When she awoke the following morning, the full impact of the events of yesterday hit her. The Flying M was sold. She lingered in bed, not

wanting, for the first time in her life, to face a
brisk spring morning. Finally, when even the cosy
and familiar surroundings did not ease the terrible
unsettledness within her, she got up.

So this is depression, she thought, staring at her
reflection in the round mirror above her old
dressing table. She ran a comb listlessly through
her short locks, her dark eyes staring back at her,
misery-filled.

'You're not such a bad looker,' Cory muttered
to herself, taking a quick inventory of her
appearance. The large dark eyes, with lashes so
long they cast a small shadow on her cheek, were
her best feature, she knew, and her freckles her
worst. Even this early in the year, they were
starting to darken over her nose. But her
cheekbones were high, and full of healthy colour,
and she remembered her home economics teacher
telling her that her heart-shaped face was the best
kind to have.

She stepped back and regarded her figure
critically. Boyish, she thought surveying the tiny
swell of her breast, the flat stomach and the long
legs. Boyish, but better than fat, she thought
severely. I think, she thought seriously, I could
catch myself a husband if I set my mind to it. She
was startled, and a little horrified, that she had
actually been considering the idea.

But realistically, she admitted, that was her one
and only way to stay in the Valley. How did I get
to be this old and not have one marketable skill?
she asked herself despairingly. She couldn't type,
or even run a cash register. What's more she knew
she couldn't bear to be trapped inside all day,
everyday under the harsh glare of fluorescent
lights.

If she was Cameron she could get a job working

on a ranch, but no one would hire a woman for the type of rugged work involved in ranching. She could get a job as a ranch cook—if she learned how to cook—but that still meant she'd be inside all day. So the only way she was going to stay in the Valley was if she married a local rancher or farmer.

'Europe, here I come,' she said blackly, going down the steps, and creeping out the front door so that she didn't have to face a repeat of yesterday's conversation with Tilda. Hearing that she was not marriageable material might be the final straw in this already bleak morning!

Morning was usually a favourite time for Cory, but today its magic was lost on her. She strode into the barn, and attached a lead to Wings' halter. The black mare neighed gently and nudged her pocket for a treat.

'Stop it!' Cory snapped, pretending not to care when the mare's head flew up in surprise at the sharp tone. 'This effects you, too, you know.'

As she led the horse out into the morning the sun was just beginning to burn the light coating of frost off the grass. Cory tied Wings to the fence and went back into the barn for her tack.

'Horses aren't very bright, you know,' she scolded irritably when she returned. She threw her saddle over the fence, unaware that the weight of the heavy stock saddle would have given most girls of her petite stature a problem.

Brushing with more vigour than was usual, she turned when she heard a vehicle on the road to see which of the neighbours was going by. 'Of course, with the munchie invasion,' she muttered to Wings, pleased to have one more thing to complain about, 'I don't always know who's on the road anymore.'

As if in confirmation, she didn't recognise the truck or horse trailer, and her curious squint became a scowl when it turned into her drive. Anyone looking for a warm reception this morning would have to look elsewhere.

Feeling markedly unfriendly, she didn't even turn from her grooming when she heard the engine shut down behind her.

'Excuse me, son.'

Cory whirled indignantly!

A cowboy she assessed, barely glancing at him before shifting her attention to the truck. A rodeo cowboy, she surmised from the array of stickers on the horse trailer, and not a very good one if the age and condition of his truck were any indication. No doubt, a drifter, just following the rodeo around the world. Naturally, his travels would lead him here, to within thirty miles of the world-famous Calgary Stampede.

Her eyes moved back to him and widened. He didn't look much like a drifter, she admitted reluctantly. His stride, long and purposeful, held the powerful grace of a large cat. His faded jeans were tight around incredibly muscular thighs, and his shirt seemed to strain to contain the bigness of his shoulders within its faded fabric.

An amused smile played across his face as he stopped in front of her. 'My mistake,' he drawled softly, his accent unmistakably Texan. 'I don't believe they make boys as pretty as you.'

Cory grimaced, but realised it wouldn't hide the blush that had leapt to her cheeks. A compliment, and a dumb one at that, she admonished herself, and here she was blusing like a thirteen-year old. Her blush heightened the tall cowboy's amusement, which was dancing openly now in his blue-black eyes. She would have loved to turn her back on him without so much as a reply, but instead her unwilling eyes were being held captive by his. Without wanting to admit it, and least of all let him see it, she was thinking how ruggedly handsome he was. A wave of thick black hair jutted out from beneath the rim of his Stetson, and feathered across his brow. His nose was straight and proud, his lips firm, his chin strong and square. But it was his eyes that were devastating. They were the midnight blue of morning just before dawn, almost purple in their intensity and depth.

Abruptly, Cory gained control of herself and rudely turned her back to him. He probably knew how easy he was to look at, Cory reprimanded herself sternly, without her mooning at him like a schoolgirl. Which, she told herself firmly, was exactly what she would be in his eyes. He looked to be in his mid-thirties.

'What do you want?' she asked, with what she hoped was indifference.

'I'm looking for a job.'

Again, Cory noticed the soft, strangely sensual, dragging of each syllable and found herself slightly disconcerted by the effect it had on her. So he had a nice voice, she scolded herself. So what?

'The foreman's gone for the day. There aren't any jobs here, anyway.' A slightly smug note had crept into Cory's voice. It wasn't normally in her nature to be petty, but somehow being able to send this self-assured stranger packing was doing wonders for her black mood.

Except that he wasn't packing. A determined note crept into the deep, soft voice. 'Maybe you could be kind enough to tell me where I can find the owner.'

His sarcasm, however softly spoken, was not

lost on her. Cory knew that she wasn't being kind at all. In an area where hospitality to strangers was unwritten law, her lack of friendliness was downright rude, and she knew it. And this morning she simply didn't care.

'Dad's at the house,' Cory retorted, turning and glaring at him. 'But don't waste your time. He never does the hiring.'

His eyes met hers squarely, and she felt again the almost electrical jolt that emitted from their dark depths. His lips spread into a slow, lazy smile that revealed teeth straight and brilliantly white against the deep wind-burned tan of his face.

'You wouldn't want to place a small wager, would you?'

'You,' Cory remarked with deliberate cruelty, 'don't look like you have a shirt to lose!'

Her taunt failed to humble the tall cowboy. His grin just widened assuredly, and he turned towards the house. He did have something about him, she admitted ruefully, as she unabashedly admired his lean form and appraised the power and grace in his stride.

Suddenly he turned, cocked a thick eyebrow at her, and winked.

Cory turned hastily back to her grooming, fuming inwardly. He had known she would be watching him! Conceited ass, she thought furiously. She took up her brushing with renewed energy, trying to block the vision of those laughing blue-black eyes.

Not totally succeeding, she gathered her equipment together and marched into the barn. With a sigh she regarded the tack room. She decided to take a few minutes to put it right, even though she knew by tomorrow morning it would look the same way. At least the darkness in the barn seemed to give some respite to her burning cheeks.

When she emerged she started indignantly at the sight of the stranger tightening the cinch on Wings with the ease and skill of long practice. She stepped instinctively back inside the door and watched suspiciously as he finished the knot and lowered the stirrup.

He took the bridle from where she had hung it on a post, and Cory watched smugly. Wings didn't like to accept the bit, and Cory had her own repertoire of tricks to get it into her mouth, but rarely did anyone else succeed at the task.

Now, to her utter astonishment, the bit slid into Wings' mouth without the least sign of struggle. Cory stalked out of the barn.

'Just what do you think you're doing?' she asked accusingly.

With a step that was too quick to evade, the cowboy was in front of her, his laughter-filled eyes resting on her face. His large hands encircled her waist, and before she could regain enough composure to protest, he had slung her easily up into the saddle.

She tossed her head angrily. 'What was that all about?' she demanded through tight lips.

'Well, ma'am,' he drawled with deliberate and aggravating slowness, 'as the new hand on this spread, I sure want to make a good impression on the boss' daughter.' He smiled engagingly and offered his hand up to her. 'Dallas Hawthorne.'

'Cory McConnel,' she returned coldly, ignoring the hand. 'Miss McConnel to you.' She whirled Wings away from the fence, noting with satisfaction that he had to leap back to avoid being knocked over. She spurred Wings into a fast gallop—but it wasn't fast enough to outrun the low and self-assured laughter of the cowboy who had been left in the dust behind her.

CHAPTER TWO

THE ride had done Cory's mood the world of good she acknowledged as she rode back into the yard just before lunch. The morning had just been too beautiful to resist, and her black mood had slowly dissipated. And finding Melissa had finally allowed her to stop thinking about that annoying cowboy.

Melissa waddled in front of her now, and Cory smiled. Melissa had been her first adopted calf, and had taken a blue ribbon in her class. She had since proved to be a superb breeder, blessing the Flying M with big, healthy calves every year. Last year, though, she'd had trouble at calfing time, and Cory decided to bring her in where she could be watched this year.

She shooed Melissa into a paddock, and swung down from Wings. The new cowboy, she noted with relief, was nowhere to be seen. Normally totally at ease with just about anybody, Cory wasn't at all confident of her ability to handle this man. Her cheeks burned anew as she remembered how lightly he'd tossed her up in the saddle.

Her reprieve from him was short-lived. When she went into the house she found Dallas Hawthorne sitting at the kitchen table, as at ease as if he had coffee with Tilda everyday of his life. He was sprawled out comfortably, his long legs stretched out beneath the table, and one powerful arm thrown carelessly over the back of his chair. He cocked his head amiably at Cory.

She ignored him, turning swiftly to Tilda. 'Do you need any help with lunch?'

Tilda eyed Cory suspiciously. 'What on earth's got into you?' she asked bluntly 'Not that I'm one to look a gift horse in the mouth,' she added quickly. 'Could you set the table?'

Cory groaned inwardly. She had rather hoped to make a salad, or something that would keep her at the counter with her back turned to the kitchen table. Dallas Hawthorne's dark and enquiring eyes had a flustering effect on her. But since she couldn't think of a way to gracefully bow out of her offer, she set her shoulders firmly and got out the utensils.

'Did you have a nice ride?' the man asked conversationally. His bold eyes met hers innocently over the rim of his coffee cup.

She concentrated on the place settings. 'Considering it got off to a bad start, it went rather nicely,' Cory replied coolly, avoiding his steady gaze.

'A bad start?' His eyes were glinting mischievously now. 'What do you mean?'

'I am not accustomed,' Cory retorted wrathfully, slamming a fork into place for emphasis, 'to being thrown into the saddle like a four-year old going on her first pony ride.' Out of the corner of her eye she noticed that Tilda had stopped working, and was listening with unashamed interest to this conversation.

'But I was only trying to be helpful, ma'am,' he purred with innocence that was given the lie by the laughter glowing in the depths of those intoxicating eyes.

'You weren't!' Cory hissed, slamming down another fork. 'You were making fun of me.'

The laughter faded in his eyes, and he shrugged his big shoulders eloquently. 'I'm sorry you took it that way,' he drawled softly.

Cory finished setting the table in silence. The cowboy's casual scrutiny made her feel self-conscious, a new and unpleasant experience for her. She breathed a sigh of relief when the last plate was safely in place and nothing had been broken. She was determined not to give Dallas Hawthorne another opportunity to laugh at her.

She was relieved, too, when Mac and the hands came through the door loudly stomping the mud off their feet and discussing a fencing operation. Mac introduced Dallas, with the explanation that he wanted the ranch to be looking ship-shape for the new owner, and that he wanted Cameron to be able to get away when his baby was born.

The hands showed what Cory thought was an annoying lack of curiosity about the new hand, and the conversation turned quickly back to fencing. And since, in her mind, he had already proved himself conceited beyond belief, she was determined not to bolster his ego by showing any interest in him, either.

She did, however, allow herself to take a guarded look at his ring finger. His fingers were immaculately clean, long, and strong and tanned, and he wore no rings. There was also no tell-tale band of white indicating that a ring had been recently removed. In spite of the fact he was an age when most men were married, Cory was not surprised. There was an air about this man, intangible and vague, that suggested total self-reliance and independence.

It wasn't until lunch was over, and the men were getting up to leave, that the new hand turned to her, forcing her to acknowledge yet another new feeling—that eyes, midnight blue and enquiring, could make her foolish heart flutter like a caged bird against her ribs.

'You have a good afternoon, Miss McConnel,' Dallas drawled casually, reaching for his cowboy hat.

For a moment Cory held her breath, pleading inwardly for the moment to pass unnoticed. But Cameron dropped his eyes, and studied his boots silently, his shoulders shaking with mirth. And Dutch hooted derisively.

'Miss McConnel!' he scoffed. 'Where on earth did you come up with that?'

Dallas' eyes met hers levelly, and the silence dragged. It serves me right, Cory thought, for telling him that in the first place. Dreading the merciless teasing that would evolve from this incident, she braced herself to have him put her firmly in her place.

'I guess I just assumed,' Dallas conceded easily, the faintest of smiles on his lips as Cory visibly relaxed.

'Well,' Mac snorted, 'you assumed wrong. This here is Cory, and I couldn't have asked for a son to be as handy and self-sufficient as she is. I guess we don't think of Cor as a girl very often—let alone a miss.'

'That's right, Dallas,' Cameron agreed. 'Cory's just one of the boys.'

Cory stared at the floor. The description was one she would have been proud of only yesterday. But today, for some reason she couldn't explain, it had a bitter sting to it. She didn't want to look at any of them, least of all into the laughing eyes of Dallas Hawthorne.

She thought they had all gone, when a strong, brown hand lifted her chin firmly, and Cory found herself looking into eyes amazingly blue, and not laughing at all, but serious and searching.

'One of the boys?' he asked so softly that she

knew even Tilda wouldn't be able to hear him. 'I
don't believe they make boys as pretty as you.'
And with a slow tip of his hat, he was gone.

The horse was magnificent, Cory thought, her eyes
fastened eagerly on him, as she rode into the yard
later that day. She wondered briefly where he had
come from, and who he belonged to, and then
realised swiftly and without question that this
horse could only belong to one man. Probably
standing seventeen hands at the shoulder, he
wouldn't seem dwarfed by the height of his
powerfully built rider.

She slipped off Wings, inspecting the horse from
a safe distance. He was a stallion, and having been
around horses all her life, Cory was familiar with
the temperament of most stallions, and instinctively
cautious around them.

'Like him?' the voice queried, almost in her ear.
She started, but her enthusiasm for the horse
allowed her to forgive, briefly, Dallas' man-
handling of her this morning.

'He's fantastic,' she enthused. 'What's his
breeding?'

'Half quarter-horse, half Hanoverian. He gets
that tremendous size from his Hanoverian father,
and quarter-horse speed from his mother,' Dallas
explained, tossing his saddle lightly astride the
fence.

'Hanoverian? That's new to me.'

'It's not very common in ranching and rodeo
circles. They're basically show horses, used for
jumping, hunter and dressage classes. I guess
they're worth a bit more than most cowboys are
willing to spend on a horse.'

Cory, with her passion for horses, felt a
reluctant alliance with Dallas. Obviously a good

horse was more important to him than the shape of his truck or the shirt on his back. It was a view Cory endorsed and sympathised with completely.

Dallas slipped through the rungs in the fence and rubbed the horse's nose affectionately and appreciatively. There was no mistaking the bond that existed between these two powerful animals.

'Come say hello to Hell Raiser,' he invited.

Cory didn't need to be persuaded. She climbed through the fence and held out her hand allowing the big horse to become acquainted with her scent. When he seemed satisfied, she moved around him admiringly, feeling the strong muscles in his legs, and stroking his back and flanks.

'He's gorgeous,' she finally breathed approvingly, turning to Dallas with a smile.

'So—you can smile,' Dallas observed wickedly.

'Of course I can smile!' she shot back instantly defensive.

'What makes you smile? Besides a nice horse, that is?' he asked sombrely, though the laughter still danced in his eyes.

She regarded him warily. Was he baiting her? Or flattering her that she had a nice smile? 'Seeing cowboys fall off nice horses usually does the trick,' she snapped, and turned and walked rapidly away from him. But she stopped in the shadow of the porch and turned back, almost against her will to watch him.

He was putting one long leg in the stirrup, and in one graceful motion he mounted the horse. She watched spellbound as he joined the others and galloped out of the yard. The great red-gold horse, even in an easy lope, was moving out ahead of the other three horses. His rider sat tall in the saddle, moving with the rhythm of the horse until they appeared to be one. Their grace, and strength, and

power melted together until they formed one
perfect, harmonious composition. Cory had been
around horses and horsemen all her life. And yet
never before, she was forced to admit reluctantly,
had she seen the teaming of horse and man
produce a picture so powerful and dramatic that it
approached art.

And later, even more reluctantly, she admitted
to listening for the pounding of hoofbeats, and
feeling strangely and ridiculously eager to see
Dallas Hawthorne again.

Why? she asked herself, when it became obvious
they weren't returning before dark. Why would
she feel eager to see him when he'd just tease her,
and make her feel silly and naïve? She allowed
herself to become indignant all over again
remembering how he'd tossed her in the saddle this
morning. On that note she stomped up to her
bedroom, quite determined that she didn't care if
she never saw him again.

But once nestled under her big, cheery, feather-
tick quilt, her thoughts returned again to him.
Where had he come from, this big, self-assured
man, with the devastating eyes? His accent was
distinctly and unmistakably Texan. But she had
taken a close look at his truck this afternoon
(when she was sure that no one was watching), and
the plates had been Wyoming. The rodeo stickers
on the horse trailer had seemed to cover every
state and most of Western Canada.

It seemed to confirm her first observation that
he was a drifter, and yet the word drifter did not
suit Dallas Hawthorne, even if it was obvious that
he was well travelled, and didn't stay in any one
place very long. An adventurer, she thought, a free
spirit—a man untamed by the conventional, or by
the status quo. What, she wondered, would make

a man like that? What would make him spurn the physical comforts of a place to call home? And did that also mean he spurned the emotional ties that came with calling a place home?

Not that she cared, she thought with a defiant, and subconscious shake of her head. She was positive that she didn't even like the man. Still, it had been rather reasonable of him not to make her look like a fool at lunch time, even though he probably thought she richly deserved to. And perhaps he had meant that remark about the smile in a nice way.

If she'd been a different girl, she realised with a touch of wistfulness, she would have handled that better. She would have smiled, and maybe fluttered her eyelashes, and said something cute and clever. She sighed. She knew she would never be able to refine the fine art of flirting—not if she practised for a hundred years. She was honest and down to earth, and if Dallas Hawthorne didn't like it, he could just go to blazes!

And what if he did like it? What if he liked her just the way she was? Maybe they could go for a ride sometime, or even just sit in the kitchen with a cup of coffee and talk. They could talk about horses, and cattle, and ranching, and dreams . . .

'What on earth am I doing?' she asked herself suddenly, and with some embarrassment. Reviewing how she felt about someone—and worse, trying to conjecture how they might feel about her—was totally alien to Cory and she felt quite resentful of this complication in her simple life.

So when she heard the kitchen door open and the hands come in, she refused to give into the temptation to go down. No doubt, Dallas Hawthorne in all his self-assured arrogance, would assume she was going down to see him—and after her flustering inner conversation she was not at all sure she could refute the fact.

Instead she lay in bed, listening with interest to the conversation that floated up the stairs. For all the apparent lack of interest the hands had shown in Dallas over lunch, it seemed they had decided to test his abilities in the one area that concerned them; whether or not he was a good cowboy.

An impromptu rodeo had developed complete with bulldogging (leaping from a galloping horse and wrestling a steer to the ground), roping and steer riding. Cory wasn't surprised to hear that Dallas had held his own.

But she was surprised to hear Dutch say to him, just as they were going out the door, 'You're one fine cowboy, son.' Dutch's admiration came hard-earned, and despite all her determination, knowing that Dallas had won Dutch's respect made her restless mind start wandering all over again.

It was a rare occasion when Cory slept in, but much to her ire, that's exactly what she did the following morning. She knew instantly what was to blame and vowed that her preoccupation with Dallas had to stop.

A day spent fishing would certainly put the needed distance between her and the overpowering cowboy, and she knew the perfect place for restoring tranquillity and regaining perspective.

It was the first time she had ridden out to the pond since the previous summer and it was more beautiful than she had remembered it. It sparkled emerald-green in the sun, and wild flowers bloomed in breathtaking abundance around it. Cory dismounted, and drank in the beauty and peace of her special place.

Already feeling decidedly calmer, she rooted

around for a nice, juicy worm, baited her hook, and tossed the line out in the water. The sun was beating down with uncharacteristic warmth for this time of year, and before long her shirt was clinging uncomfortably to her back. The calm waters of the pond looked tempting.

Cory considered briefly how cold the water would be, particularly because the pond was filled with melted snow from the mountains. She decided she was too hot to care. No one would be within miles of this spot today, so she unselfconsciously slipped off her clothes and plunged into the pool.

She shrieked with delight at the impact of the freezing water. She dove and ducked and swam energetically in an attempt to keep the effect of the icy water from touching her too quickly. Finally, nearly blue, and with chattering teeth, she decided to surrender.

She turned to swim for shore, and gasped. Dallas Hawthorne, leaning lazily on his saddle horn, was watching her with unapologetic interest. She stopped, treading water on the spot. How long, she wondered desperately, had he been there?

Dallas smiled calmly and raised a hand to the brim of his cowboy hat in a gesture that struck her as being absurdly casual considering the circumstances.

'Get out of here!' she shouted at him, her visions of sitting and having coffee with him shattered by her swift and indignant annoyance with the easy-going expression on his face.

'And if I don't?' he responded calmly, shifting slightly in the saddle but making no attempt to move.

'I'll freeze to death before I'll come out with you sitting there,' she promised stubbornly through chattering teeth. The gall of the man! The unabashed arrogance! How could she have lain awake most of the night thinking about him?

He shrugged, unmoved by her threat, his gaze not wavering from her face.

Her skin was beinning to feel numb from the cold water, and Cory realised she couldn't make her threat good. Her anger became tinged with a touch of panic. 'Would you at least turn around?' He didn't answer and she became increasingly frightened that he really intended to watch her emerge from the water.

'Dallas,' she begged, hating herself for the pleading note, 'please? I'm freezing.'

With a mock mournful expression he turned the big horse away from her, and Cory swam speedily to shore, not once taking her eyes from his broad back. She hesitated briefly when her feet touched the rocky bottom and she had to stand up.

'Are you going to look?' she asked nervously.

'Of course,' he called blandly over his shoulder. She heard what she could only hope was a teasing note, and scampered quickly over to her clothes, and then retreated hastily behind a bush. She pulled on her clothes with clumsy fingers that trembled with rage and cold.

'What are you doing here?' she stormed, coming out from behind the bush fully clothed and fixing him with her most accusing stare.

'Looking for mermaids,' he replied calmly, turning back towards her, his eyes resting unperturbed on her flushed face. 'It's one of my favourite pastimes, though I must say this is the first time I've found one.'

'You shouldn't have watched!' she admonished angrily.

He smiled down at her off the big horse, not the

least intimidated by her anger. 'Give me a break, Cory. There isn't a man alive who wouldn't have watched.'

'Well,' she sputtered indignantly, 'most would have shoved off when they were asked to.'

His widening grin informed her that he wasn't 'most', and she would have happily slapped his face if they had been at the same level.

'You didn't answer my question,' she reminded him sourly. 'What are you doing here?'

'Looking for Melissa. She broke out of the paddock this morning. She's probably looking for a nice quiet place to have her calf.'

Cory struggled for a moment, torn between anger with him and concern for her cow. She decided her anger was quite ineffectual anyway. 'Wait. I'll come with you,' she offered resignedly. Quickly she retrieved her fishing pole from the pond.

She whistled softly and Wings ambled over to her. Cory swung into the saddle. 'See,' she pointed out haughtily. 'I can do it all by myself.'

'But it's not nearly as much fun, is it?' Dallas drawled, grinned at her scowl, and then changed the subject. 'Which way do you think Melissa would go?'

'The thickets west of here are probably a good place to start,' she replied with cold dignity, starting Wings in that direction.

'How's the fishing?' Dallas asked conversationally, as if the fact he had watched her swimming stark naked was already the farthest thing from his mind.

'Not great this morning,' Cory commented, relieved Dallas wasn't going to tease her. 'You can get a fair-sized rainbow trout out of there most of the time.'

'What do you use for bait?'

'Just worms.'

'And you bait your own hooks,' he guessed drily.

Cory shot him a disdainful look. 'Of course. Did it look like there was anyone there to do it for me?'

Dallas chuckled softly. 'A real tomboy, aren't you Cory?' His voice lost the teasing note and became serious. 'But I think maybe you have to work at keeping that tomboy image intact. Underneath it, I'm willing to bet there's a woman urging you to let her grow up. A woman who's feminine, and vulnerable,' he paused and looked at her intently, 'and passionate.'

Cory met his searching gaze and looked away quickly, pretending to be concentrating on the trees for signs of Melissa. 'I think,' she returned uneasily, 'that you should mind your own business, which is being a cowboy.' She touched her heels to Wings' sides and surged ahead of him.

Raiser pulled up beside her, keeping pace easily. 'You can't run forever,' Dallas stated quietly.

Couldn't she? she wondered, realising that by asking that question she acknowledged running. Acknowledged that sometimes late at night she did wonder what it would feel like to have strong arms wrapped around her, and to have the voice of the man she loved whispering gentle things in her ear. Acknowledged it and was frightened of this unknown thing—love, and yes, passion. Frightened enough to stay with somebody like Timmy who was unthreatening, and safe, and secure.

Not at all like this man beside her who suddenly made her feel more threatened than she had ever felt in her entire life, though she had no intention of letting him see that.

'Would you just drop it?' she snapped, and to

herself she added, I'm not ready for a man like you, Dallas Hawthorne.

Dallas shrugged, and then pulled his powerful mount to a quick halt. 'Did you hear that?' he asked Cory, scanning the trees.

She shook her head, but then she, too, heard a faint and powerful bawl. Dallas spurred Raiser through the bush towards the noise. Cory followed at a more cautious pace, breaking into the thicket to see Melissa trying valiantly to get to her feet, and then with a huge sigh, sinking back down.

Dallas was off Raiser and stripping off his shirt in the same liquid motion. Quickly and expertly he examined the cow.

'She's broken water,' he observed tersely. Without hesitation he slid a muscular arm inside her. 'Damn. Cory, the calf's in backwards. We're going to have to pull him. Cory?' He glanced over his shoulder, and was at her side in an instant. Gently, he pulled her from the saddle.

'Sorry,' he apologised mockingly. 'I know you like to do things yourself.' He regarded her pale face. 'Are you all right?'

'I'm sorry,' she stammered, wavering. 'It always does this. You'd think having grown up around——'

'For God's sake, Cory,' he cut her off impatiently, 'even tomboys are allowed a few human weaknesses. You don't have to apologise to me for them.' The cow bellowed and he took Cory's arm firmly. 'Sit here,' he commanded, suddenly businesslike. 'Do what you can to keep her calm.'

Cory nodded numbly. 'You'll be fine, Melissa,' she whispered woodenly, fighting nausea.

Later she looked up, and found it impossible to turn her eyes away. Even through the fog that threatened to engulf her, came a deep and admiring awareness of his magnificent body. The muscles in his arms and chest were powerful and well-defined, knotting and rippling as he strained to pull the calf. The sweat was beaded and shining like oil against his bronzed, taut skin, and glinting like tiny diamonds in the thick curling hair on his chest.

I'm not ready for a man like this, she repeated to herself, but was unable to deny that a sensation like craving tingled in her belly.

Suddenly Melissa relaxed, and Cory knew with relief that the calf had slipped out. Dallas ran his hands carefully over the spindly little legs and smiled, his face made even more handsome by the sudden and fleeting tenderness in his expression. He gathered the wet little bundle in his arms and deposited him gently at Melissa's head. Then he sank down beside Cory and threw a casual arm over her shoulder.

'Are you okay?'

She smiled weakly, uncomfortably aware of the electricity of his touch. 'I'll live.'

They watched in appreciative silence as Melissa cleaned the calf, then nudged it insistently to get up. The calf tested its wobbly legs, fell and tried again. Finally he was up, and Melissa struggled to her feet. Eagerly the calf searched for milk, found it, and sucked contentedly. Cory sensed, without looking at Dallas, that he was feeling the wonder and magic of this new little life every bit as deeply as she was.

Dallas rose and looked with a grimace at the blood drying on his skin and jeans. 'I'm going to have to go for a dip in your little pond.' A glint came into his eyes. 'Why don't you come?'

Cory missed the glint, still watching the calf. 'I'd love to, but I don't have a bathing suit.'

The devilish light grew in his eyes. 'Neither do I,' he responded softly, and then laughed when the crimson flared in Cory's cheeks. 'See you at lunch, little innocent.' He swung lithely into his saddle.

'Dallas.'

'Change your mind?' he teased, one dark eyebrow lifted with amusement.

'No.' She hesitated. 'Would you mind not mentioning the part about me nearly fainting to anyone?'

The playfullness died in his eyes, and they darkened with annoyance. Without answering he whirled the big horse and galloped away.

Cory mounted Wings and let confusion engulf her. She had known, of course, that he wouldn't tell anyone, and she knew the remark had been deliberately calculated to irritate him. To push him away from her because his remarks about her being a tomboy had been altogether too personal and too perceptive, and because there had been a challenge there that was more than a little frightening. To push him away from her because in his handling of that calf she had seen an exquisite tenderness that she was sure he didn't show the world very often. To push him away from her because his arm thrown lightly and casually across her shoulders had stirred a tiny flame within her, and she was positive it was a response he did not share.

Careful, Cory, she warned herself firmly, careful.

She recognised Timmy's truck in the yard and quickly put Wings in her stall and went up to the house.

Timmy met her on the porch. 'I was hoping you'd be back soon. I'd almost given up hope.'

'I wasn't expecting to see you for awhile,

Timmy. You must be up to your eyebrows in work.' In her own mind she recognised that she sounded mildly unenthused about his unexpected appearance, but Timmy didn't seem to notice.

'I had to go into the Valley to see about a tractor part.' His tone grew slightly reproachful. 'I saw the sign on the gate. It was a hell of a way to find out, Cory.'

Funny, she thought, that she had never thought to call him. The events of the past few days, and especially that tall, attractive, and extremely aggravating cowboy, had completely erased Timmy from her mind. She eyed Timmy now, and her mind automatically compared the two men. Not really men, she corrected herself. Dallas was a man, Timmy was a boy. Oh, she knew that he was legally adult, but suddenly he seemed gawky and young. He was slim to the point of boniness, and she doubted that even time would fill Timmy out. His face, for all his thinness, had a child-like roundness to it, and always looked shiny like it had been freshly scrubbed. His short blond hair was neatly combed back, except for the untameable rooster tail at the top of his head.

'I'm sorry. I don't know why I didn't call you. I guess I just didn't feel like talking about it yet.'

Timmy accepted this with his usual easy-going grace. 'How about tonight? We could go have a beer in the Valley.'

She felt an odd reluctance to be with Timmy tonight, and found herself answering, 'Gee, Timmy I really wanted to wash my hair tonight.' The words trailed off lamely and Cory was astounded that she could have said anything so incredibly banal. Timmy, thankfully, didn't seem to be put out by her excuse, even if in her own ears it had the ring of a terribly bad old joke.

The stairs creaked, announcing the presence of a third party and Cory turned to see Dallas, his hair still curling wetly from his swim, sauntering across the veranda. She could tell from the half-smile that played across his lips that he had overheard her. His cocky look assured her that no woman would dare to give him such a half-baked excuse, but then Cory was positive that he hadn't been on the receiving end of very many excuses.

Cory fully intended to let him pass into the house unintroduced, but he stopped expectantly. Grudgingly Cory introduced them.

Dallas extended his hand. 'How are you, son?'

Though Cory felt acutely the weight of unspoken tension between herself and Dallas, Timmy seemed blissfully oblivious to it. He grinned openly and accepted the hand. 'I'm just fine, thanks. Good to meet you.'

His friendliness, Cory thought unfairly, but with irritation, reminded her suddenly of an eager puppy. Dallas' use of the word son had not passed over Cory either. Whether he had used it intentionally or not, she had no idea, but it made her even more painfully aware of what a kid Timmy was. And what did that make her, she wondered with confusion? In Dallas' eyes was she a kid, like Timmy, or was she the woman that Dallas had implied she might be? Dallas met her puzzled gaze easily, but she could find no answer in the inky blue of his eyes.

'Timmy,' she blurted out impulsively, 'stay for lunch. I'm sure it's almost ready.' What was she doing, she wondered uneasily? Surely, she thought fearfully, she wasn't trying to make Dallas jealous? She dismissed the thought swiftly. More likely she wanted to impress upon him that some people took her quite seriously. Relieved with this explanation, she followed Dallas and Timmy into the house.

Whatever her motivation, she soon regretted it. Timmy, far from being attentive, talked to Mac about farming all through lunch. Fertilisers, crop rotation, and farm machinery held little interest for Cory, and she had the same edgy, bored feeling that had always encompassed her during a science lecture at school. Everyone else joined in the conversation with what seemed to her to be ridiculous enthusiasm.

Except Dallas. He ate his dinner in silence, then lit a thin brown cigar, and looked absently out the window while he smoked it. Cory kept hoping he would rescue her from this dreadful conversation by mentioning Melissa and the calf, but he didn't. Finally she caught his eye, and raised her eyebrows in question. He shook his head ever so slightly and she realised with frustration that he had no intention of breaking up the ongoing conversation. Despite her muffed role in it, she was going to bring it up herself, when Dallas excused himself quietly, got up, and left. Certain that no one would notice she slipped outside after him.

'I thought you'd tell them about Melissa and the calf,' she chided. She had intended to sound conversational and casual, but even in her own ears it came out sounding like an accusation.

Dallas feigned surprise. 'I didn't want to interrupt the stimulating conversation about Massey Ferguson tractors to mention something so mundane as a calf being born.'

'Mundane? It wasn't mundane.' She looked at him narrowly. 'That's not the reason at all. You did it to punish me.'

'Punish you?' A slight smile tugged at the corners of his mouth. 'You mean listening to your boyfriend ramble on about farming is punishing? Why would I want to punish you anyway, Cory?'

'Because I hurt your feelings when I asked you not to tell anybody about me fainting. I underestimated you, and you want to get me back.'

He looked at her squarely, his lips a tight line. 'I think you're underestimating me again,' he commented dangerously, and Cory was so startled by the change in him that she almost forgot what they were talking about. His face was stony and his eyes glittered with pure ice. Intuitively and suddenly, she knew there was something in Dallas, a history that she had played no part in, that was in his eyes now. And then as quickly as it had appeared, the animal anger disappeared, as though it had come instinctively and then reason had chased it away.

'If you weren't upset with me, why didn't you mention Melissa at lunch?' she challenged cautiously.

'I thought the experience was good for you,' he informed her, the strange intensity so completely evaporated that it might never have been.

'Good for me?' Cory was baffled. 'I've never been so bored in my life.'

'Really?' Dallas growled, his tone soft and steel-edged. 'Be a barrel of laughs being Mrs Timmy Stubbs, wouldn't it?'

'Mrs Timmy Stubbs?' she croaked, stunned. 'Me and Timmy? Dallas, we're just friends.' Why am I explaining this to him? she wondered. Why does it seem so important that he know?

His face was impassive. 'You should ask Timmy if that's what he thinks,' he suggested coolly.

'Don't be absurd! Of course that's what he thinks.'

'I think that Timmy is in love with you.'

Cory had had enough of this ridiculous and altogether too personal conversation with this arrogant cowboy. 'For your information,' she hissed, 'I don't give a damn what you think about anything!'

He was at her in one long stride. Cory found her shoulders locked firmly in a painfully strong grasp. For a moment she felt pure panic, afraid of losing her heart and soul in the depths of those midnight eyes. Then she relaxed under his firm grip, accepting. Accepting what? she wondered dazedly. His face moved closer to hers, and for a stunned and strangely exhilarating moment Cory thought he was going to kiss her. But then with a slow smile he released her, and cocked his head at her arrogantly.

'You do give a damn what I think,' he noted with insufferable assurance.

She watched as he turned and walked away, and then the lethargy left her and anger replaced it. 'You're the most conceited bastard I ever met!' she shouted at his retreating back. Immediately she clapped her hands over her mouth, unable to believe she had said that. The sudden silence in the kitchen told her that everyone had heard her, and she blushed wildly. To add to her confusion and embarrassment, she could hear Dallas' soft, mocking laughter floating up over the yard to her.

CHAPTER THREE

'WHAT'S going on between you and that guy?' Timmy demanded possessively as they stood at his truck after lunch.

'Nothing,' Cory denied, injecting a false note of brightness into her voice. 'He just gets under my skin, that's all.'

'You let me know if he's bothering you, Cory. I'll fix him.'

Timmy's bravado was almost laughable, and indeed Cory would have laughed if Timmy wasn't looking at her so seriously. How, she wondered, did Timmy think he would fix Dallas? Fight him? Dallas would flick Timmy away with little more effort than it took him to flick at a bothersome fly.

'You remembered we're going to the Valley social on Saturday didn't you?'

'Of course I did,' she lied, the dance having completely slipped her mind until he mentioned it.

She was completely unprepared for his next move. He planted a damp and awkward kiss on her mouth, and then blushed to the roots of his short hair. 'See you Saturday,' he promised shyly, then embarrassed, he hopped into his truck and roared out of the yard.

Cory stared after him. What was wrong with him? she wondered. Or was she just looking for tell-tale signs because that idiot Dallas had suggested Timmy was in love with her? She sighed. There was probably nothing wrong with Timmy. It was her own head that didn't seem to be screwed on right today.

Still, the kiss worried her. It had had no effect on her, except that she felt a sudden urge to wipe her mouth. What worried her was that Timmy should do something like that. It implied that the situation she had been so comfortable with for so long was in danger of changing. Cory didn't think that there was anymore chance of being romantic with Timmy than with a basset hound. And didn't they say that love destroyed the best of friendships? But she admitted ruefully that falling in love with Timmy Stubbs would certainly solve some of life's little problems.

She turned back to the house and noticed that Dallas was at the corral saddling up for the afternoon. His back was to her, but she knew with a sinking heart that he had witnessed Timmy's spontaneous kiss, and for that matter, probably caused it. And though she had told herself she wasn't ready for a man like Dallas, and had sincerely meant it, for some inexplicable reason she didn't want him to think she was romantically involved with anyone else, either.

'I'm going into town,' Cory called into the kitchen, plucking a set of truck keys from their hook on the porch.

'The Valley?' Tilda asked, coming on to the porch and surveying Cory curiously.

'No, Calgary. I need a dress,' Cory replied carelessly.

Tilda's mouth fell open, but she quickly closed it again. 'Of course. A dress,' she echoed, her eyes twinkling with merry inner knowledge.

Cory gave her a withering look and stomped off the porch. A dress, she told herself turning on to the highway and putting the accelerator of the ancient pick-up to the floor.

'I must be the only girl in the world who would

get a strange look because she wanted a dress,'
Cory muttered defensively to herself. Then
realising, sheepishly, that it was a little out of
character for her, she set about convincing herself
that this sudden desire for a dress had nothing to
do with *him*.

'I need a dress,' she told herself firmly. 'I knew
at Christmas that I was hopelessly out of date.'
She had been the only younger woman at the
Valley Christmas dance wearing a floor-length
formal. 'The length is cocktail, dear,' she mimicked
the well-meaning old matron who had felt it was
her duty to let the poor McConnel girl know what
was going on in the world beyond the Flying M.

So cocktail it will be, she told herself grimly half
an hour later, when the impressive Calgary skyline
became visible from the highway.

She pulled into the first large shopping mall,
sending a small thank you heavenward that it was
so close to the southern edge of the city. Cory had
learned to drive on deserted country backlanes,
and her confidence behind the wheel quickly faded
with the complications of driving in the city.

Cory caught a glimpse of herself in a store
window as she entered the mall. Her decision to
buy a dress had been impulsive, and she hadn't
even bothered to change from her ranch clothes.

'I hope "cowboy" is still vogue,' she muttered to
herself, not really aware that there was a difference
between her faded Levis and designer jeans,
between her plaid shirt and one edged with silk
fringes, and between her worn leather cowboy
boots, and high-fashion Western boots.

Three stores and twenty-two dresses later, Cory
was beginning to wonder wearily if she would ever
find a dress to suit her. She dismissed, immediately,
the thought that she might not usually be so fussy.

Though she knew it was out of her price range, she casually walked into Marcelle's, a high-fashion designer boutique. The dress caught her eye immediately, and she knew, wistfully, it was the one. She fingered the filmy fabric longingly, knowing how well the pale peach would set off her healthy colouring. But three hundred dollars?

'You like it, no?' a petite French saleswoman asked, coming up behind her.

Cory nodded. 'I love it. But I can't. It's just too much money.'

The French woman smiled. 'Try it on.' She saw Cory's hesitation. 'Treat yourself,' she insisted, pressing the dress into Cory's arms, and shooing her into a fitting room. A few minutes later she passed through nylons and a pair of delicate, peach open-toed shoes. Cory eyed the two-and-a-half-inch heels with a nervous giggle.

The dress was perfection, Cory thought as she stared with awe at her reflection in the mirror. It was a handkerchief style—the top a filmy loose square that tied narrowly at the shoulder, emphasising the soft and seductive curve of her shoulder. The skirt was two layers of the same fabric, each ending at a different length. The dress, Cory thought headily, made her look unbelievably sophisticated. And the higher heels, she noted with delight, gave her height that made her look like a leggy New York model.

'Please, come show me,' the saleswoman invited from outside the door.

Shyly, Cory emerged from the dressing room.

The woman's hands flew to her cheeks. 'Ooooo,' she exclaimed. 'You are a vision. Turn.' Cory turned awkwardly.

'No—like this.' The little woman executed a pirouette, and Cory imitated her. The dress floated around her in an enchanting cloud.

The woman's eyes were dewy. 'Every girl,' she enthused firmly, 'must once in her life own such a dress. This dress it makes you an angel and a seductress all at once. You must have it.'

Cory opened her mouth to protest, then watched in horror as the woman flipped up the hem and pulled a single thread from it.

'The dress is damaged. I will sell it for half price.'

Cory gasped. 'No. I couldn't. The dress isn't damaged. I can't take it for half price. It would be dishonest.'

'Fine,' the woman stated with a mischeivous smile, 'if you won't take it for half price, I will give it to you. I am Simone Marcelle. I own the shop.'

'Oh,' Cory said, feeling foolish. 'Of course you can't give it to me. I'll be happy to pay half price for it—if you're very sure?' she finished uncertainly.

'Of course I am.' The little woman sighed. 'If you could see what some of my creations look like on the people who buy them you would more readily understand. It will be tremendous advertising. Besides, it does my heart good to see one of my dresses look so wondrous. You make the dress a magic thing—ah, and to sell such a dress to a young woman on the brink of love!'

'On the brink of love?' Cory echoed, feigning innocence, and yet somehow knowing it was true that there was something about her now that hadn't been last week. Still she wasn't prepared to admit that mysterious 'something' had anything to do with love.

'It's in your eyes,' Simone Marcelle smiled gaily. 'So, you don't know yet? That, too, is part of the human condition. Our foolish heads get in the way of what our hearts try to tell us.' She flicked a hand at Cory. 'Go change now.'

On the brink of love, indeed, Cory thought, half-amused and half-annoyed, as she turned the truck homeward. Twice in one day! Dallas thought she was in love with Timmy—she frowned. No, that's not what he'd said. He said Timmy was in love with her. And she wasn't in love with Timmy.

If she was going to fall in love, which she wasn't, she'd fall in love with—she stopped herself abruptly. Love, she told herself firmly, is for other people. I've got enough problems, without that.

'Tilda,' she called, sailing into the house a little while later. 'Come see.'

A few minutes later she was proudly modelling her dress for a properly awed Tilda.

'Mac,' Tilda shouted excitedly out the bedroom door. 'Mac, come here.'

Mac burst into the room. 'Where's the fi——' and stopped mid-sentence his eyes growing wide. And then his shoulders slumped.

'When did you grow up, Cor?' he asked, unable to disguise the sadness in his voice.

'Dad!' she cried in horror, as a single tear squeezed out of his eye and slipped down a weathered cheek.

He sat down on the edge of her bed, and Cory put a comforting arm around his shoulder, seeking the wisdom of Tilda's eyes above his head. Tilda just smiled and shook her head.

'I'm sorry, Cor, I don't want to spoil your dress for you. It's just,' he searched for words, 'Tilda has been trying to tell me you're a grown woman, but I don't know, Cor. You always looked the very same to me. She'd say that one day, and the next day I'd see you come bouncing across a field on that black horse of yours, and I'd think to myself that you didn't look any different than when you were twelve.

'And you never do the things grown women do, Cor. I mean you don't fiddle with your eyes, or pour smelly stuff all over yourself before you go out.

'But just then, when I came in, you looked so much like your mother did the first time I saw her. And she wasn't no little girl. She was your age, but I saw her as a woman. And now,' he concluded sadly, 'that's exactly what's going to happen to you. Some handsome man's going to come along, and he's going to see you as a woman, Cor. And he's going to take you away from me.'

'For heaven's sake, Dad! It's a dress. It's not going to change me to put on a dress.' But the words were forced, because in the back of her mind she could hear a voice drawling, 'underneath it, I'm willing to bet there's a woman'.

'That you would pick a dress like that means you've changed, Cor.'

'Now, Dad,' she soothed, 'don't go worrying about any handsome men—I don't know any.' But again Dallas Hawthorne materialised in her mind. 'That I care for, that is,' she amended hastily.

Mac and Tilda exchanged a glance, and Cory looked from one to the other not quite grasping what it meant. Mac got up and moved to the door. He took a long look back at her, and a trace of the old sparkle returned to his eyes.

'You do look beautiful,' he admitted gruffly.

Cory watched as the door closed behind him. She turned to Tilda mystified. 'I can't believe all that was because of a dress!'

'Neither can I,' Tilda responded softly. 'I suspect it's more because of——' She stopped herself abruptly. 'More because of something else,' she finished weakly. She gave Cory a little pat on the shoulder and left.

Cory eased out of the dress cautiously. 'It seems to me,' she informed the dress uneasily, 'that everyone on this earth knows a secret—except me.'

Cory stood on the porch and waited, with a touch of impatience, for Timmy to arrive. It was a beautiful night, she thought, taking another deep breath of the cool air, and lifting her shining eyes to the merrily winking stars.

Her fingers moved appreciatively to the silky fabric of her dress, and she shivered. She had never looked so wonderful as she looked tonight she thought without conceit. Nor felt as wonderful either. It was magical what a fabulous dress could do for a girl's soul. She felt like a fairy godmother had waved a wand and proclaimed her a princess for the night. Without, she reminded herself lightly, all the complications of pumpkins and glass slippers.

A small light flared and died slightly behind her, and she started. Then the pungent, familiar aroma of a cigar filled the night air. Out of the corner of her eye she could make out the shadowy outline of Dallas' tall, powerful figure, and with an effort she did not turn to him.

'I didn't see you there,' she murmured, feeling the colour burn in her cheeks as she imagined the fool she must look, gazing at the stars and stroking her dress lovingly.

'I'm glad,' his quiet reply came out of the darkness. 'If you would have seen me, you would have gone back inside.'

She couldn't deny it. Since the day that Timmy had been over for lunch she had carefully and deliberately avoided finding herself alone with Dallas. She had recognised then that she was attracted to him like a moth to a flame and her instinct for self-preservation made her wary of giving anyone the power to singe her wings.

And Dallas, she became more and more certain, would singe her wings. She saw him daily at meals, of course, and was more aware of him than she wanted to be. Of his physical presence, the muscles so hard and lean that she could see their outline even beneath his work clothes. Of his face, so ruggedly handsome, and of his eyes that made her feel like a flustered, gauche schoolgirl everytime they rested on her face.

But it was something that she couldn't see that made her wariest of all. Dallas, in bits and pieces, told them about himself. He told richly warm and funny anecdotes about the rodeos he'd been in and the ranches he'd worked on. But there was an element missing from those stories. He never mentioned his childhood, or a family, or a girl who had been special to him.

For a man who exuded such overpowering virility and rugged sensuality Cory found it disturbing that a woman's name never slipped into his conversation. Was he a Casanova, incapable of deep feeling and commitment? Or had he been burned so badly that he avoided relationships altogether? Either way it made her attraction to him a dangerous thing. Because she firmly and old-fashionedly believed that commitment and caring had to go hand-in-hand with chemistry.

One other incident lingered in her mind like a hazy warning. One night Dallas had sat through dinner unusually quiet and withdrawn. After, he had stared out of the window, drawing slowly on his thin black cigar. Thinking what, she didn't know, but she knew in his face in those brief unguarded moments she had glimpsed a hardness and a coldness that were awesome and impenetrable.

'I think I will go in,' she stammered, these thoughts racing through her mind. 'Timmy won't be here for awhile, and it's starting to feel cold out.' She turned quickly from the porch railing.

'Don't.' He emerged into the soft glow of the porch lamp, blocking her path, and looking down at her with eyes that were unreadable in the night.

'You look beautiful enough to kiss, Miss McConnel,' he drawled softly, and Cory thought she heard a mocking note in that deep, somewhat devastating voice.

'Dallas, please don't tease me,' she pleaded, staring at the cracked old boards of the porch floor. To her horror, her voice was trembling.

'I'm not teasing.'

Her eyes flew to his face, and indeed there was no laughter in the eyes that held the blue-black colour of the night, though a light like fire burned in their depths.

Her eyes dropped again from his and her heart began to flutter wildly. With an effort she found her voice. 'I want to go in, Dallas. Let me by.'

'No,' he breathed in a tone now devoid of softness. 'You're still running, Cory. You're still running away from the woman you are meant to be. Is it because you know I can show you, that you've been avoiding me?'

Don't do this to me, Dallas, she wanted to scream into his confident appraising face. Don't show me all I can be, and then just walk away. But she couldn't say it. Words like caring and commitment deserted her and she was left only with a deep yearning burning like a fire out of control somewhere near the centre of her being.

He accepted her muteness as answer. A small wicked smile played across his lips, and a note of challenge appeared in that deep drawl. 'You want

me to kiss you, don't you Cory? You want me to
show you the way a woman should be kissed.'

The awkwardness left her and she disguised her
near panic with swift anger. 'Your conceit is
remarkable,' she snapped icily. 'No, I don't want
you to kiss me. I'm quite sure that a kiss from you
would be far less exciting than some of the other
kisses I've received.'

His laughter was soft and vaguely cruel. 'I don't
think you've ever been kissed.'

'I have, too!' Cory spat the words at him.

He moved closer and Cory backed quickly away
from him. With lightning-like swiftness he snared
her wrists and pulled her harshly back to him.
'Afraid?' he asked, lifting an amused eyebrow.

'No,' she said with conviction she was far from
feeling. She tried vainly to twist from his hold, but
knew herself to be physically at his mercy. 'Let me
go, Dallas,' she pleaded, her voice a faint and
frightened whisper.

'No,' he refused softly. His arms moved around
her locking her into his embrace. He pulled her
more tightly against him, and her heart started
pounding at the searing heat that radiated from his
muscular and unyielding length.

She stared up at him, wide-eyed, and understanding without wanting to, that the trembling within
her body was not fear alone but also that terrible
yearning, like a thirst that demanded to be
quenched. She struggled, not just against him, but
against herself, and then the struggle became too
much. The fight went out of her like the air out of
a needle-pricked balloon.

He felt her suddenly relax against him, and
chuckled softly and with unforgivable assurance.
'Do you want to be kissed, Cory?'

She hated him at that moment with a rage she

had not known that she possessed. Hated him for the sudden warmth that enveloped her, and for the tingling expectation that touched her like the spray from a waterfall. Hated him with every fibre of her being for the incredible power that he so arrogantly wielded over her. She hated him desperately—but not desperately enough to say no.

'Yes,' she whispered, beaten. 'Yes, I want you to kiss me.'

His eyes mocked her surrender, as if he had known her answer could be no different, and then his mouth descended on hers, his lips hard and demanding. Ruthlessly, he explored the contour of her lips, bruising them, demanding that they respond to him. Her lips, to her shock and horror, obeyed the command of his. They parted gently, meeting his eagerly and shyly. And then even the shyness was gone, and her lips, unbidden, returned the passion of his.

And then the nature of his kiss changed, becoming tender and inquisitive; welcoming her. Something in the depths of her being was awakening, and Cory felt her soul begin to soar as she answered the ancient call to womanhood. She felt as though she were on fire and floating at the same time. The sensation within her was deeper and infinitely more exhilarating than a cool pond on a warm day. Something inside her shook off eagerly the sleep of childhood, tentatively and then boldly stepped through the invisible door that he held open for her.

She felt, her mind teased her from faraway, just as he had promised she would feel. She felt like a woman.

The sudden, stark illumination of headlight beams glanced off them, forcing her to surface, unwilling and gasping, from the waves of passion that had washed over and over her with seducing pleasure. She jerked away from Dallas, but was unable to break the bond with his eyes, which were faintly puzzled as if something in that virgin kiss had startled him and left him slightly shaken. The expression was gone, replaced swiftly with a gaze hooded and derisive.

Dallas glanced without interest at the truck and then turned his eyes back to her flushed face. 'Well?' he demanded coolly.

He was insufferable, she thought, not daring to look at him. 'It was no big deal, Dallas,' she lied softly, turning swiftly from the indifferent scrutiny in his eyes to watch the truck pulling to a halt.

His laughter was soft and disbelieving, but without comment he, too, turned his attention to the truck.

He watched it with narrowed eyes. 'You can't ever be happy with him now,' he promised with cold satisfaction as Timmy emerged from the truck.

She turned startled eyes to Dallas, but his expression remained remote as he watched Timmy Stubbs come up the stairs.

'Evening, Timmy,' he drawled casually, his voice betraying nothing. Cory felt a wave of relief, not realising that to an astute observer her own flushed face would reveal everything.

Timmy's eyes flew from her face, to Dallas', and back to hers.

'I was keeping Cory entertained,' Dallas informed him, the edge of boredom in his voice so sharp and unmistakable that Cory felt it twist through her with knife-like pain. It had been a game, she thought dully, just a stupid, cruel game.

The suspicion faded from Timmy's eyes and he beamed at her. 'You sure look nice tonight, Cory.'

Dallas' eyes moved lazily over her. 'She does, doesn't she?' he commented with no apparent conviction. Cory stared at him, aghast at his callousness. She felt as though she had been brutally used, found wanting and dismissed. Save for Timmy's presence she would have burst into tears. She searched his face, hoping for reprieve. He glanced at her briefly and coldly.

'Have fun, kids,' he offered nonchalantly, and with a casual wave, and the confidence and indifference of a large cat he sauntered away.

'Are you ready, Cory?' Timmy asked.

With difficulty she looked away from the broad back that was fading quickly into the night and forced a bright smile at Timmy's anxious expression. 'Yes,' she said, 'yes, I am.'

But as the truck pulled out of the drive she gave in to the urge to look back, just once, at the place where they had stood entwined beneath the soft light of the porch lamp and the moon.

'I thought you didn't like that guy,' Timmy finally blurted out when the silence between them had become uncomfortably long.

'I don't!' Cory snapped with such feeling that Timmy glanced sharply at her.

'Then how come you were out there with him?'

'Timmy,' she admonished, with exasperation, 'he happens to work for us, and he happened to be on the porch. It was no big deal.' It was the second time tonight that she'd used that expression she reminded herself. It was also the second time she'd lied. She sighed.

'Let's just forget it and have a good time,' she suggested a little tersely.

And that's exactly what I intend to do, she told herself with firm resolve as they parked the truck in front of the community hall. She placed her arm through Timmy's and they strolled across the parking lot towards the bright lights and laughter of the community hall.

In a quick survey of the cheerfully decorated hall Cory picked out Cameron and Shelly and decided that their light-hearted kind of company was exactly what she needed to survive this evening. Timmy's company alone would have left far too much room for introspection.

Cameron's eyes widened with disbelief as they approached the table.

'Cory,' he stammered, 'is that really you?'

Maybe that's why Dallas had kissed her, she thought grimly. Maybe he'd mistaken her for someone else and then discovered it was just good old tomboy Cory in a dress.

'It's really me,' she said with the faintest note of apology.

'Well, I'll be damned!' Cameron exclaimed with a grin.

'Cameron!' Shelly gave him a playful smack. 'That's no way to tell a girl how nice she looks.' She turned her sparkling eyes to Cory and smiled warmly. 'You look lovely.'

Cory smiled gratefully and sat down beside her. Timmy and Cameron went in search of refreshements, and Cory soon found it impossible to remain depressed under the steady flow of Shelly's cheerful chatter, and particularly because Shelly told her at least four more times how nice she looked. By the time Timmy and Cameron returned, she was looking around the hall with some hopeful anticipation of enjoying the evening in spite of Mr Dallas Hawthorne.

For once, she realised a trifle smugly, she looked incredibly fashionable. Her gaze stopped at Nancy Jacobsen. Nancy was already surrounded by ardent admirers. She was wearing a simple black sheath, that was slit seductively to the thigh.

Normally, Cory admitted, she would have been envious not only of Nancy's dress, but of the flair that she wore it with. But not tonight. Cory appraised the older girl's dark beauty thoughtfully, and knew with a sudden thrill that she rivalled it. Nancy was all seductress. Cory thought of Simone Marcelle telling her that she was seductress and angel too, and smiled, feeling some of the inner confidence she'd enjoyed earlier returning.

Shelly nudged Cory, and pointed at the door. Cory watched with amusement as Mac, looking for all the world like a mother hen leading a flock, came in followed closely by Dutch and Shorty. Mac always claimed that a hundred wild horses couldn't get him to a community dance, and yet Cory couldn't remember him missing even one. Shelly nudged her again.

'Who is that?' she asked with unveiled interest.

With a sinking feeling, Cory followed Shelly's gaze to the door, and stared stunned at the figure who filled it. She had known from Shelly's tone who it was going to be, but she hadn't been prepared for such a transformation. Gone were the faded work clothes. His suit had a subtle Western cut, its blue only a shade darker than that of his eyes. It had been tailored to fit perfectly over the broad expanse of his shoulders, and even Cory, with her lack of knowledge about clothes recognised the cut was expensive. The grey, high-crowned Stetson was pulled low over his brow, and was immaculate, as were the shining dress cowboy boots.

'It's Dallas,' Cory murmured, striving not to betray with her tone how intoxicatingly handsome she found him, or how distraught his unexpected appearance made her feel.

'That's Dallas?' Shelly responded admiringly. 'You didn't tell me he was so nice looking,' she teased Cameron.

'That's because I knew you wouldn't think he was anywhere near as handsome as me,' Cameron responded lightly, squeezing Shelley's hand.

Shelly giggled. 'And of course he isn't.'

Cory smiled at the little interchange. Now that was what love was she told herself firmly. What Dallas had forced her to feel earlier had nothing to do with love. It had been passion, an instinctive, animal desire completely separate from emotion. At least for him. It didn't seem that easy for her.

None the less, if she had been asked at that very moment to explain what she felt for Dallas, without hesitating she would have said hate. She wondered what word he might use to describe his feelings about her, but unable to face the possible answer, she impatiently brushed the question from her mind.

She rejoined the conversation with Shelly, unable to prevent herself from watching him from under the silky curtain of her long lashes. He sat with Mac, but he was obviously restless. He scanned the room, his eyes coming to a stop on Nancy. They narrowed assessingly and coldly like the eyes of a hunter, confirming her worst suspicions about him, which she was rather startled to find she didn't want confirmed.

He unfolded himself from his chair and unhesitatingly crossed the room to her. He cut through the throng around Nancy Jacobsen with casual confidence, bent over the raven-haired beauty's shoulder and whispered something in her ear. Nancy swung around to face him with obvious anger; anger that faded quickly into a lovely and enticing smile as she appraised the dark stranger.

'I'd give my eye teeth to know what he said,' Shelly chirped, watching the scene with interest. Cory could only nod, watching him with shadows of pain darkening her expressive eyes. Bitterly she wondered if he'd told Nancy she was pretty enough to kiss.

Dallas pulled back Nancy's chair and extended a hand to her. She placed her hand in his and they made their way to the crowded dance floor.

'What a beautiful couple,' Shelly noted with a touch of awe. 'Honestly, they're like something out of a fairytale.'

It was true, Cory acknowledged grudgingly. The crowded dance floor seemed to become a ballroom belonging only to them. They fitted together like two pieces from the same puzzle, and that kiss that Cory had shared with Dallas only an hour ago seemed like a terrible joke.

Nancy, sophisticated, and suave, and mature, was the type of woman that Dallas could truly enjoy kissing. Nancy would know what to say to him, and how to respond to him. Nancy would be unfettered by a commitment to old-fashioned virtues. Cory could see that in the way they were dancing together, and gazing, with a touch of wicked promise, into each other's eyes.

For some reason, that look filled Cory with a dull and aching sense of loss and regret that wouldn't go away.

CHAPTER FOUR

CORY accepted Timmy's invitation to dance, hoping that it would help to break through the cloud of gloom that had shrouded her ever since Dallas and Nancy had taken to the floor. She succeeded in that Timmy was a terrible dancer, and keeping her toes out from under his enthusiastically stomping feet took a good deal of skill and concentration.

But when the set ended, she found to her dismay they were wedged in firmly right next to Dallas and Nancy. She searched frantically for a way out but there was none. With resignation she faced a brightly smiling Nancy.

'Cory!' Nancy exclaimed with friendliness that didn't quite reach her black eyes, 'how nice to see you.' Her eyes quickly scanned Cory, and narrowed briefly with surprise. 'Don't you look sweet?' she asked lightly.

'Thank you,' Cory replied coolly. 'You look very "sweet" yourself.' Her emphasis on the word sweet was scathing, and Dallas' laughter was low in his throat, like a rumble. But when Nancy turned to him with questioning eyes, his face was deadpan.

She looped a possessive arm through his. 'How do you stand being at such close quarters with this handsome devil?' she asked Cory crooningly.

Cory met Dallas' eyes and looked quickly away. How do you? his mockingly crooked eyebrow had seemed to ask.

'Actually,' Dallas interceded smoothly when Cory seemed unable to answer and Nancy was obviously delighting in her discomfort, 'it's more the other way around.'

'What do you mean?' Nancy asked sharply.

Dallas regarded Cory intently. 'I mean,' he drawled softly, 'that I have trouble being at such close quarters with Miss McConnel.'

Nancy scanned his face uncertainly, and then laughed a little brittly. 'What a delightful sense of humour. Don't blush so, Cory. He was just kidding.'

Nancy brushed by Cory with her head high, but Dallas released her hand and stood looking down at Cory. 'I wasn't,' he denied softly, and Cory's heart stood still, as he gazed down at her with vaguely troubled eyes. And then abruptly, as though he'd found the answer to some inner question he struggled with, he strode away.

Another of the suave, lady-killer cowboy's lines? she wondered furiously as she watched him walk away. She wanted with every fibre of her being to believe that, and was dismayed when she couldn't convince herself. Had he felt something, too? And if he had, why was he behaving the way he was?

Was it possible he was afraid? she thought and was startled. The thought was incongruous. Dallas, so powerful, so self-assured, so virile—afraid? Of a slip of a girl like herself?

Impossible, she told herself firmly, and yet suddenly she could visualise him with that hard, cold look on his face that she had glimpsed once after dinner. A man wasn't born with an expression like that. It was a scar just as surely as ridged and purpling flesh. Had it been love that had left that scar, Cory wondered? Could love be that punishing?

The music started again, and to Cory's relief someone cut in on Timmy before he had a chance to comment on what Dallas had said. From then on she could barely remember who she was dancing with. No sooner would one dance stop than another young man would be asking her eagerly to dance with him.

She smiled until she wished she'd greased her teeth, and laughed and chattered as though she was having the most wonderful night of her life. But deep inside she knew it was all a show, and recongnised in her behaviour a juvenile 'I'll show you attitude' that she didn't care for—and couldn't stop.

Involuntarily, over and over again, she sought him out. He wasn't hard to find, his height and stature making him stand out from the crowd. She noted with satisfaction that he had deposited Nancy back at her table, and was now twirling a more nondescript young lady around the floor. Her satisfaction steadily became edged with irritation as she realised that he fully intended to dance with every unattached female in the room— ranging in age from six to sixty.

Even Missy Henderson, a little girl confined to a wheelchair because of cerebral palsy, wasn't missed. Dallas swooped her out of her chair, and whirled around the room carrying her effortlessly in his strong arms.

A break came and Cory sank breathlessly into the chair beside Timmy, who favoured her with a dark look.

'You and Dallas,' he commented sulkily, 'seem to be competing for the grand prize at a popularity contest.'

'What an odd thing to say!' Cory reproved impatiently. 'Honestly, I thought you'd be relieved. You hate dancing.'

'Well, I'm thinking of taking some lessons,' he

said with a trace of meekness that Cory found aggravating. His eyes were round and serious.

'Timmy, you don't even like to dance,' Cory pointed out practically, aware that her voice held a trace of irritation that she hadn't intended for it to hold.

'But you do, and the way things are going tonight, I may never see you if I don't learn.' There was a tiny rebuke in his seemingly casual statement.

Cory studied Timmy with sinking heart. He was watching her ardently, his large eyes full of admiration, and perhaps, she admitted slowly, something more than admiration lurked there. When had that happened, she wondered, and how had she missed it?

The sudden 'May I join you?' interrupted her train of thought. Cory recognised the deep timbre of the voice without looking up. But even if she hadn't, the sudden hostile look in Timmy's eyes would have told her who had materialised at their table. Cameron offered Dallas a chair and introduced him to Shelly.

'Are you from Texas, Dallas?' Shelly asked when the introductions were completed.

Dallas nodded, and Cory could have sworn that a hooded curtain fell smoothly over his eyes. But if it had meant to be discouraging, it had failed. Shelly had every intention of satisfying her natural small-town curiosity.

'What about your name? Is it real?'

Dallas laughed. 'I'm afraid so.' He hesitated almost indiscernibly. 'My mother was a war bride from England. She'd never seen anything like the State of Texas, and she loved it with an enthusiasm that even most Texans can't imitate. I was named in honour of her favourite city.'

'But you grew up in the country?'

Dallas nodded. 'On a cattle ranch. The old expression that cowboys aren't made, but born, is true of me.'

'What brings you so far from home?' Shelly asked, unashamedly interested in him.

The pause was pregnant. 'Texas hasn't been home for a long, long time, Shelly.' His voice was even and casual, but Cory was startled by the sudden clouding of the sky that was his eyes. Sadness? she wondered, or had it been resignation? For the second time that evening, Cory found herself wondering what memory haunted Dallas. A girl, with shining hair and laughing eyes and a sweet, husky voice?

Cory shook her head, chiding herself for this ridiculous speculation. The look had already vanished from his eyes. She might have even imagined it. She became aware of Timmy addressing her.

'Cory, I'm hot. Let's go outside.' His tone implied that he was none too thrilled with their present company.

'Good idea,' Cory responded stiffly, as if she too was not overly impressed with the company, when in fact she was more intrigued than ever by the mystery of the confident, complicated man who sat across from her. She was annoyed that, in spite of all her efforts, her attraction for Dallas would not quit. Quickly she followed Timmy out the side door of the hall.

'Hmmm,' she sighed, striving for sincerity. 'It's still lovely out.'

'Cory, I need to talk to you.' Timmy's voice was low and urgent.

She shifted her attention from the stars to his earnest face. His gaze moved self-consciously from hers, and he studied the parking lot over her shoulder.

'Cor, I don't want you to go to Europe with your Dad.' His voice was slightly hoarse.

'That makes two of us,' Cory responded lightly. 'I don't have any choice, Timmy.'

'Yes, you do.' He hesitated, and then took her hands so tightly in his that it hurt.

'You could stay here with me, Cory.' His eyes met hers again, wide and eager, and a little frightened.

Dallas would certainly be pleased with his timing if he knew what was transpiring out here, Cory thought dazedly.

'Marry me, Cory.'

'Timmy . . .' she breathed gently.

'Don't say no, Cory. Please.' His voice held a desperate note. 'I know you don't think you love me. I didn't think I loved you either, not until I thought about you going away. And then I knew that I wanted you to be with me all the time. I can't let you go to Europe. I'd miss you too much.'

Life with Timmy wouldn't be so bad, Cory thought dully. It would be just like it was now. Peaceful and secure and familiar. And the Valley would be hers forever. Wasn't that what she wanted, more than anything else?

'Timmy,' she said cautiously, 'this doesn't mean yes, but I want you to kiss me.'

Awkwardly and eagerly Timmy took her by the shoulders and his lips met hers. He held his stiff kiss for a lengthy minute, then stepped back and regarded her with shining eyes.

Cory could have cried. Chalk another one up to the cowboy, she thought miserably.

Timmy sensed her reaction and began to talk fast. 'Look, Cory, don't tell me tonight. Take a few days and think about it. I'm sure you'll start to understand how good it could be for both of us. Will you do that?'

She could stay here, she thought wildly. She could raise horses, and have Timmy's babies. The romantic side of marriage probably wasn't what it was cracked up to be anyway. Timmy would make a good husband. He'd be dependable and hard-working and not overly demanding. And he'd make a wonderful father. He'd be gentle and playful—she stopped herself. She could almost hear that deep, mocking voice. You can't ever be happy with him now.

'I'll think about it,' she told Timmy bleakly, and shivered.

'You're cold,' he announced protectively. 'Let's go in.'

Dallas was still at the table when they rejoined them. He'd been laughing about something, and his laughter-filled eyes met Cory's boldly. Her heart warmed at how the laughter had chased the shadows from his face. But the expression faded as his eyes moved from her pale face to Timmy's shining one, and then back to hers. He cocked his head slightly, his eyes suddenly narrow and questioning. She felt ridiculously and helplessly as though she had somehow betrayed him. Her gaze slid away from his, and for a moment he looked grim. But then, as though he had shrugged mentally and dismissed both her and Timmy, he turned his attention back to Shelly and Cameron.

'So when are you two getting a little spread for that bambino of yours to run wild on?' he asked casually.

Shelly sighed wistfully, and Cameron looked uncomfortable.

'Sorry,' Dallas apologised quietly. 'I didn't realise it was a bad subject.'

'It's not a bad subject,' Shelly assured him quickly. 'It's just the impossible dream right now. My husband's a cowboy,' she continued proudly. 'That's what he's good at, and that's what he's happy doing. I wouldn't want it any other way. But right now we're paying rent in town, and that makes it hard to save for our own place.

'Someday, though, Cameron's going to be a foreman. And when the baby's big enough, I'm going to get a job, too. We'll have our spread someday.'

Dallas smiled at her. 'I'm sure of it,' he responded. The music started again, and Dallas excused himself without even favouring Cory with another glance. Cory felt suddenly incredibly weary. The popularity she'd enjoyed earlier lost its appeal entirely. Timmy wanted to marry her. She wanted to deny to herself that a week ago her decision would have been easier. But then a week ago, all of life had been easier. Because a week ago there had been no Dallas Hawthorne, holding out a brass ring for her, and when she reached, lifting it tauntingly and cruelly beyond her grasp.

She watched him in mute anger as he continued to make his rounds of the dance floor. He's going to ask every single girl here to dance—except me, she realised dully. Why? If the kiss had meant nothing he'd ask her to dance just like everybody else, wouldn't he? What, she wondered slowly, if it had really meant too much? Dreamer, she scoffed at herself.

She was relieved when the band took another break. The music was beginning to give her a headache; the music, and the weight of Timmy's unexpected proposal, and maybe especially the weight of *his* presence.

'What's wrong, Cory?' Shelly asked quietly,

touching her arm, her observant eyes taking in Cory's pale face with concern.

'I have a headache,' Cory admitted reluctantly, praying silently that those observant eyes wouldn't guess the reason.

'Let me find you an aspirin,' Cameron offered.

'I would have got it,' Timmy protested with a small pout, after Cameron had gone, and Cory felt her exasperation with him growing.

A slurred 'Hello, there,' caused Cory to look up. Shorty hovered drunkenly over their table and Cory groaned inwardly. He pulled up a chair and made himself comfortable.

'How's Cameron's little woman?' he asked loudly.

'Fine thanks,' Shelly responded coolly.

Shorty made an elaborately hurt face. 'Are you mad at me because I've been working Cameron so hard?' he wheedled. Shelly's eyes met his disdainfully, but she didn't reply. Shorty reddened and his expression became quite ugly. 'You're sure a snooty one,' he growled. He reached out and grabbed Shelly's hand. 'But I know all about you, and you ain't got any right to be snobby have you?'

Cory stared at him stunned, and Shelly paled, and tried to twist out of his grasp.

'I know why you got married,' Shorty said smugly. Cory gasped in horror, and tears welled up in Shelly's eyes as she searched the room desperately for Cameron.

'Shorty, you shouldn't talk like that,' Timmy rebuffed, blushing like an ineffectual school ma'am.

'No, you shouldn't. Let go of Mrs Scott's hand.' The softly drawling voice was cool and dangerous, and Cory's relief was immediate. A situation that had seemed to be in danger of running out of control, she was suddenly confident was in complete control.

But for all that, there was something rather frightening about Dallas in that moment. Though not a muscle moved in his impassive face, Cory could sense a tension coiling within him, a tension coupled with a chilling calm. Her suspicion that something hovered in Dallas' past that had been cruel was confirmed in the stunning, if controlled, expression of ruthlessness that showed in the taut lines of his face.

Shorty dropped Shelly's hand like it was hot, and twisted in his chair to face Dallas.

'I think you had better apologise to the lady,' Dallas suggested, his voice soft and calm, but his eyes icy with threat.

Shorty was too far gone to notice, and his thin lips curled into a sneer. 'No cowboy who works for me is going to give me orders.'

'I stopped working for you at five o'clock this afternoon, and I don't start again until six o'clock on Monday morning. Apologise.' The drawl was deceptively soft and silky, but there was still no missing the command or the threat inherent in it.

'And what are you going to do if I don't?' Shorty challenged.

Dallas flexed a strong arm lazily. 'Don't push me, Shorty,' he warned softly.

Shorty seemed to suddenly recognise the threat and the sobering reality of what he'd said to Shelly. 'Sorry,' he mumbled to her with obvious embarrassment, though Cory couldn't be sure if his embarrassment was because of his remarks to Shelly or because he'd been forced to back down. He rose awkwardly and stumbled away.

'Thank you,' Shelly said to Dallas, her voice quavering.

Cameron appeared and set two white tablets in front of Cory. He looked around the table with growing concern. 'What's going on?'

'Nothing,' Shelly denied, close to tears.

'It was Shorty——' Timmy was silenced with an impatient look from Dallas.

'What about Shorty?' Cameron looked into Shelly's pale face. 'What did he do to you, honey?' he demanded. Shelly said nothing and Cameron scanned the room with angry eyes. 'I'm going to kill him,' he threatened in a low, determined voice.

'Cameron, do yourself and your wife a favour and forget it,' Dallas advised steadily, and with an impressive air of command. 'He was drunk. He's already apologised, and a fight is going to land you in more trouble than it's worth.'

Strange advice from a man who hadn't hesitated to use a less than subtle threat of violence himself, Cory, thought, but then recognised with clarity something unspoken in that advice. It was as if Dallas was no stranger to violence or its price, and he wanted to protect the younger man from some dark lesson that he had learned.

I sound worse than a dime-store detective novel, Cory chided herself, but was relieved when Cameron considered and then agreed.

The music was starting again and Cory didn't feel she could bear it. 'Timmy, I think I'd like to go home.'

They were at the truck before she realised that she'd forgotten the aspirin on the table, and asked Timmy if he would go back for them.

She climbed into the truck and waited, shutting her eyes against the pain pounding in her head. But she opened them when she heard a stifled giggle followed by a low, familiar laugh. Through the darkness she could make out two forms, and even in the darkness it was unmistakable who they were. Nancy and Dallas. Cory shut her eyes again when his head dropped over Nancy's and she disappeared within the embrace of those powerful arms.

Don't think about it, she commanded herself bleakly, but she couldn't help it. She thought of his kiss and the fire it had started within her, and as much as she despised him, she knew, had he taken her in his arms again, she would have been just as eager, just as lost. He was an incredibly dangerous and puzzling man, she acknowledged wearily.

Timmy climbed into the truck and handed her the aspirin and a paper cup full of water. She swallowed them, hoping that they would work quickly on the terrible pounding in her head, and wishing they could work on the terrible chaos in her heart.

The ride was silent, but then Cory had closed her eyes to discourage Timmy from talking to her. She didn't feel like talking, she thought. Not about the proposal, not about Shorty and least of all about Dallas Hawthorne.

When they pulled into the yard she gave Timmy a quick, wan smile and then slipped out of the truck before he could even attempt to repeat his performance of earlier.

Once in her room, she looked thoughtfully at herself in the mirror. 'Mrs Timmy Stubbs?' she asked the reflection, and then frowned. She didn't look like a Mrs Timmy Stubbs should look. Mrs Timmy Stubbs should look exactly like Timmy's mother, all round and dimply and rosy.

She wouldn't make a very good Mrs Timmy

Stubbs, either. Because in order for her to be a good Mrs Timmy Stubbs, something in Cory McConnel would have to die. And she knew what that something would have to be—it would have to be the passionate part of her that an arrogant cowboy had coaxed to the surface for the first time tonight.

She sighed and pulled the dress over her head and put on her pyjamas. She glanced back into the mirror. 'Mrs Dallas Hawthorne?' The question startled her, and then she laughed shakily. But as she climbed into bed and closed her eyes, Mrs Dallas Hawthorne kept running through her head like a haunting and sad melody.

'Cory, it's time for church.'

Cory shook herself awake and looked at her clock. 'Give me a minute, Tilda,' she called back.

Even a shower hadn't shaken the lethargy she was feeling and she wondered if she was coming down with something. Like Texas 'flu, she thought with grim humour.

'Cory, you look terrible,' Tilda confirmed, laying a plump hand against Cory's forehead. 'No fever. Are you feeling all right?'

'Sure. I just didn't sleep very well. And I had a bad headache last night.'

Tilda raised an eyebrow intuitively. 'How was the dance?'

Cory sighed. 'Rotten,' and then she offered a hasty explanation so that Tilda wouldn't be left any room to guess the real reason it had been rotten, 'Shorty and Dallas had a bit of a tiff.'

Tilda didn't look surprised. She nodded her head. 'I could see that coming. What was it about?'

'Shorty said something pretty nasty to Shelly. I

don't think he meant it. He'd just had too much to drink, and his tongue got away from him. Dallas made him apologise.'

Tilda chuckled. 'Good for Dallas, though I somehow doubt we've heard the end of that.'

'Tilda,' Cory hesitated, 'Timmy asked me to marry him.'

She waited for Tilda's face to light up with joy and was amazed when it mirrored only concern.

'What am I going to?' Cory wailed.

Tilda sat down and laid a reassuring hand over Cory's. 'Do you love him?' she asked quietly, her eyes intent on Cory's face.

'How do I know?' Cory hedged. 'I'm comfortable with him. We get along well. You know, we've never even had a fight!' In her own ears she sounded like a salesman pushing a mediocre product with forced enthusiasm.

Tilda smiled patiently. 'Usually a few sparks fly when people love each other, Cory. Love is a strange thing—it peaks all the emotions, not just the tender ones. Love is hate and anguish and confusion, as well as tenderness and exhilaration and delight.'

'Tilda, I don't think I love Timmy,' Cory admitted bleakly.

'I know, sweetie, I know.'

'So what am I going to do?'

'I can't answer that for you, Cory,' Tilda said, her brows knitting together. 'That's one decision we all have to make alone.'

'If I married Timmy I'd be content, even if I don't love him. I'd be able to stay here, and work with horses, and——'

'A marriage of convenience?' Tilda queried softly. Cory nodded. 'Your whole problem is that you don't know what love is. If you did, I don't

think that you could ever choose contentment over
it.' She paused. 'It doesn't seem like you to be
thinking of using Timmy like that.'

'I wouldn't be using him, Tilda. It's what he
wants.'

'Timmy doesn't know what he wants, Cory.
He's just a boy. Don't cheat him of having a
chance to fall in love. Don't cheat yourself.'

Cory mulled that over thoughtfully. 'I suppose
you're right, Tilda, but I still have to think it
through really carefully. My whole future is at
stake here.'

On a brighter note, she added, 'Tilda, if Mom
would have been here I think she would have said
the very same thing you said. Thank you.'

'Don't make me cry before church,' Tilda said
with a sniff. 'I only wear make-up once a week,
and it would be a shame if it were running down
my face.'

Cory laughed and gave Tilda a warm embrace
at the same moment that Mac began impatiently
honking the horn outside. She followed Tilda to
the door and then stopped short.

'Is he going?' she grumbled, eyeing the large
figure already settled comfortably in the back of
the station wagon. 'Who invited him?'

'Cory! Dallas came in this morning and said
he'd like to go.' Tilda chuckled. 'He says he likes
to sing.'

'He could sing here,' Cory muttered, but
squared her shoulders and marched out to the car
behind Tilda. Tilda climbed into the front seat,
and Cory toyed with the idea of climbing in beside
her, leaving Dallas in the back of the car by
himself. But he was already out of the car,
gallantly holding the door open for her. She slid
into the back seat without looking at him.

Mac was doing a boisterous rendition of *Shall We Gather at the River* and his voice effectively covered Cory's whispered, 'Atoning for last night's sins?'

Dallas looked at her curiously.

'I saw you leave with Nancy.'

'Jealous?' he asked mildly.

'Certainly not!' Cory snapped and turned her attention out the window.

Dallas used the cover of Mac's voice as effectively as she had. 'I'm thinking of taking a picnic lunch down to the pond this afternoon. Care to join me?'

Cory turned and eyed him warily at this unexpected invitation. Her eyes were drawn to the firm, slightly upturned line of his lips. and for a moment she felt almost dizzily compelled to say yes. Then she remembered, with bracing indignation, that he hadn't even danced with her last night—and that he'd left with Nancy. What kind of game was he playing?

For one brief, ecstatic moment she thought of him looking down into her face last night and saying softly 'No, I'm not,' in answer to Nancy's taunt that he'd been kidding about being attracted to her. Was it possible that something about her appealed irresistibly to this self-possessed man beside her? She searched her mind frantically for what it might be, and came up sadly blank.

Far more likely, she thought unhappily, that after her inexperienced return of his kiss, he'd relegated her to a comfortable kid-sister position, and gone off in search of someone older, and wiser and more dynamic to vent his passion on.

Kid-sisters might be taken on Sunday afternoon picnics if older brothers weren't doing anything more interesting. She remembered the look in his

eyes when she had come in with Timmy last
night—all-seeing and disapproving, just as an
older brother's might have been.

Dallas was waiting for her answer.

'I don't think so,' she said stiffly, though a part
of her already mourned that decision.

He shrugged with aggravating confidence. 'We'll
see.'

'Go to hell!' she hissed.

He laughed. In Cory's mind it sounded just like
how an older brother would laugh at a little sister
in a rather difficult stage of growing up.

After the service, the ladies' guild had tea, coffee
and cookies waiting at the back of the church.
Cory slipped away from Dallas, hoping fervently
that he would feel like a bump on a log standing
by himself in this gathering. But her neighbours
betrayed her with their unaffected friendliness. She
glared at him nastily, cursing his natural ease from
her position by the coffee urn.

But even as she cursed him, she couldn't help
but notice how well he fitted in with these honest,
earthy people who were her friends and neighbours. For a reason she wasn't at all inclined to
investigate, she was glad he was, like her, one of
them. She felt her studied indifference sliding
away, and then knew sinkingly it was gone all
together when she saw his eyes rest on Missy,
sitting alone in her wheelchair by the door. Those
eyes that could be so stunningly and mysteriously
cold, held only gentle compassion now.

Unhesitatingly he extracted himself from the
circle and went over to the little girl. Cory found
herself straining to hear what passed between
them.

'Hello, Mr Hawthorne,' Missy said shyly.

'Now what's this Mr Hawthorne stuff?' Dallas

asked gently, crouching down beside her. 'All the pretty girls just call me Dallas.'

Missy giggled happily.

'I bet you'd like to do some visiting, too, wouldn't you?'

Missy nodded eagerly, and Dallas scooped her up into his arms. Cory watched fascinated, as the tall cowboy made his way back into the social circle as if it were the most natural and normal thing in the world to have a little girl clinging possessively to his neck.

She felt a stab of tenderness for Dallas that she didn't want to feel. So he had some saving graces, she thought, annoyed at how swayed she could be by them. So what? But the glowing face of Missy Henderson threatened the sincerity of her inner conversation.

Suddenly he was beside her, gazing down at her fiendishly over Missy's head. 'Missy,' he said, his eyes never leaving Cory's face, 'how would you like to go for a picnic with Cory and me this afternoon?'

Cory's jaw dropped, and the protest rose indignantly in her throat, then died unspoken. The joy in the fragile little girl's face was so precious and hopeful.

'Really?' Missy squeaked. 'Mama!' she shouted shrilly, and curious eyes turned to them. 'Mama, I'm going on a picnic with Dallas and Cory.'

Cory saw the approving looks and smiles and met Dallas' laughing, triumphant eyes with a resigned, uneasy grin.

'Chalk another one up to the cowboy,' she said weakly.

CHAPTER FIVE

MISSY snuggled deeper into Dallas' chest, her eyes heavy from the huge lunch she had just eaten, and from all the excitement of her first horseback ride.

'Dallas,' she said, her voice faintly hoarse from screaming 'faster, faster,' while they had galloped, 'would I have liked you when you were a little boy?'

Dallas chuckled. 'I don't think so, sugar. I was a real brat.'

'No!' Missy protested.

'Yup. I used to torment a pretty little girl who looked a lot like you by putting snakes in her desk and tying her hair to the back of her chair.'

Cory smiled, hugged her knees to her chest, and gazed out over the pond. She was glad that she was here, and even willing to forgive the trickery Dallas had used to get her to agree to come. The puzzles, the tension and the antagonism had seemed to melt away under the bright early summer sunshine, and under the flow of Missy's never-ceasing chatter.

On the ride out there had been places where the trail narrowed, and riding abreast of Dallas and Missy her leg had brushed up against his. Riding at his side and feeling that pressure had felt so right somehow. And Dallas had looked down at her with a half-smile that seemed to confirm he was feeling the same warm and wonderful good feelings.

Dallas seemed different this afternoon, in a way Cory had trouble pin-pointing. He had always struck her as being relaxed, but it seemed to go so much deeper right now, as if he had let go of something—an ingrained guardedness—and was as totally at ease with himself and with her as she had ever seen him. What dark secret did he guard? she wondered, shivering at the memory of the dangerous man she had glimpsed at the dance last night.

'Are you cold?'

She turned and looked at him, and was stunned by the jolt of tenderness that ran through her. Missy was sleeping, cradled gently in his powerful arms, her expression trusting and contented.

Cory was taken aback by the sudden physical ache of wistfulness that washed torturously over her. For a lifetime of afternoons like this one. For it to be their child with her nose pressed possessively into Dallas' chest.

What was she saying to herself? she wondered wildly, almost panicking under the scrutiny of his dark eyes. What if he could read her mind?

It wasn't true, she told herself firmly. It couldn't be true. She hadn't known him long enough. She didn't know enough about him. And yet even as she tried to convince herself, she saw him in her mind's eye as she had seen him that very first time. Her heart knew. Even then.

'Cory, what is it?'

His brow was furrowed with concern, and she realised she was trembling slightly and that the blood had drained from her face. It took every ounce of discipline that she possessed not to lean closer, and offer her lips to him—not to murmur, 'I just realised I'm in love with you.'

He was cruel, she told herself desperately. He had been deliberately cruel last night. He hadn't even danced with her . . .

'Why did you kiss me last night?' she finally asked, concentrating hard on a blade of grass she twirled between her thumbs, and congratulating herself on how calm, how casual she sounded.

'Because you looked enchanting,' he replied with disheartening matter-of-factness.

'But not enchanting enough to dance with?'

His expression was faintly sardonic. 'You were with your boyfriend, Cory, who happens to be wearing his heart on his sleeve right now. And after arriving to find you alone and blushing prettily with another man, it probably wouldn't have taken much to make him feel backed right into a corner. I didn't want to give him any excuses to come out fighting.'

She sighed. He'd handled that brilliantly, even managing to come out of it looking quite altruistic. But she still didn't have a clue how he felt about her. She hesitated, and then played her last card.

'Timmy,' she said watching him closely, 'asked me to marry him.'

He looked like maybe he had already guessed that, but his eyes narrowed grimly on her face. 'Don't do it, Cory,' he advised tersely.

'Why, Dallas?' she asked softly, an unspoken hope leaping crazily within her.

His gaze was unrelenting and unreadable. 'Cory, I like Timmy. I think he's decent and dependable and honest. I just don't like him for you.'

'Why?' she persisted.

'Oh, hell Cory!' he ejaculated with a trace of impatience. 'I don't know why and it's really got nothing to do with me.'

The hurt welled up inside her. It had seemed for a minute that he might say something that would give her reason to hope, to believe these powerful, illogical, uncrushable feelings stirring within her were shared by him. Instead, he had pulled so swiftly away, establishing himself as an only slightly concerned stranger.

He seemed to sense her hurt and he sighed. 'Cory, maybe I've just seen too many people get married because the other person is a pleasant habit, and they can't see anything else to do, or any other place to go.'

'A trap you've managed to escape, I see,' she commented stiffly.

'I've had a close call or two,' he admitted, with complete lack of emotion or regret.

She wanted so badly to be indifferent, but she had to know. 'So what happened?' She glanced at Missy. 'You obviously like kids.'

His expression softened as he, too, looked at Missy. 'I like kids.' His face became inexplicably hard. 'Parents have an awesome responsibility, don't they?'

Cory thought she heard the faintest of bitter notes. 'I don't think that's a responsibility that many of them abuse, Dallas,' she said softly.

Dallas looked at her thoughtfully, as if he wanted to tell her something. Something she suspected would explain that bitter note and perhaps more. But then his expression grew closed, and he shrugged, and shook Missy gently awake.

'Raiser is faster than Wings,' Missy informed Cory with obvious pride, on the ride back. 'Raiser is the fastest horse in the whole world, isn't he, Dallas?'

'Well, maybe not in the whole world, sugar.'

Missy gave Dallas a disapproving look. 'In the whole world,' she insisted stubbornly. 'That's what I'm going to tell my teacher tomorrow. I bet she'll ask me to tell the whole class.' She looked slyly at

Cory. 'And Dallas is the nicest man in the whole world. And the strongest. And the handsomest. Isn't he, Cory?'

'Well, maybe not in the whole world,' Cory responded lightly, imitating a drawl.

'He is, too!' Missy replied, glaring at Cory. 'If I was eighteen instead of eight, I'd marry him. Are you going to marry him, Cory?'

Cory could feel Dallas' eyes resting on her with wicked amusement. 'I don't think so,' she murmured uncomfortably, avoiding his gaze and feeling immediately mortified that she hadn't said a vehement no. She stole a glance at him, expecting him to be grinning, and was disconcerted to see he, too, looked uncomfortable.

Had Dallas somehow guessed what she was feeling for him? she wondered with horror. Was his discomfort that of a school teacher who had just discovered one of his students had a crush on him? The sudden silence between them was only slightly less notable for all Missy's chattering.

'Cory,' Dallas said softly, as they watched Missy and her mother drive out of the yard.

She turned to him, and he pushed a strand of wayward hair off her face, his eyes steady and searching on hers.

'A long time ago,' he mused, almost to himself, 'I stopped believing there were people who were honest and innocent, and sensitive and caring.' He touched a finger to her lips when she opened her mouth to ask why, his eyes remaining intent on hers.

'Don't think,' he warned gently, 'that you're going to make a believer out of me.' Abruptly he swivelled on the heel of his boot and walked away.

She stared after him in confusion. Had he been

warning her not to love him? Trying to tell her that he'd been hurt and that it wasn't going to happen again? And by telling her that, wasn't he also admitting in a back-handed sort of fashion, that he felt more strongly than he wanted to?

But if the latter was true, he certainly fought it. In the next days there was a marked change in his attitude towards her. If that kiss beneath the porch light had ignited a fire in him, as it had in her, he kept it carefully hidden. And if he was sometimes haunted by its memory late at night, it didn't show in dark smudges under his eyes as it did with her.

His attitude towards her was polite and friendly, and yet vaguely distant. She found herself wondering bleakly sometimes if he'd joined the others in considering her just one of the boys.

It was crazy to have fallen in love with a man who didn't want to be loved, but try as she might to fight her feelings, they only deepened with each passing day. He was in his element with horses, and Cory often drifted down to the corral to watch him breaking and training a filly that she and Mac had given up hope on. He was incredibly gentle and firm with that high-spirited young mare, and his results were astounding. Sometimes he'd ask Cory to help, and she'd feel so close to him after those laughter-filled, exhausting afternoons. And though he complimented her sincerely and readily on her feel for horses, and for the quickness with which she learned, there was never any indication that this was the same man who had once complimented her in a far different way.

He was also emerging as a natural leader. There didn't seem to be anything about horses or cattle or ranching that Dallas didn't know. Shorty, who had been chilly with him since the dance, grew chillier as Mac and Dutch and Cameron turned more and more to him for information and advice on various ranch problems.

She loved him for all that, and for more. For the way he could tease Tilda into fits of girlish giggles. For the way he walked with those long confident strides, for his voice, soft and deep and firm, for the colour of his eyes, different with his shifting moods.

She knew, too, that it had been wrong to consider marrying Timmy when she knew she didn't love him, it was doubly wrong to consider it when she was deeply and desperately in love with someone else. Reluctantly she called him.

He sat on the porch swing beside her now, swinging it vigorously.

'It's because of him, isn't it?' he asked softly of her refusal.

She was startled that she was so transparent, but there was no sense denying it. 'Yes.'

'Does he love you, Cory?'

She knew she should have said no. And yet she intuitively sensed a deep struggle in Dallas. Occasionally, she would look up from her dinner to find his eyes resting on her, grave and tinged with the same kind of muted light she had seen burning in them the night he had kissed her. And she would sense in him a deep and self-imposed loneliness, and her heart would ache for him.

'I don't know,' she said, and felt close to tears. She remembered looking at Dallas once and wondering how punishing love could be. Somehow she had the feeling she was finding out.

Cory stared grimly through the darkness at her bedroom ceiling. In three hours, she'd probably relived those words over dinner a thousand times, and still couldn't make any sense out of them.

Cameron had been talking about the filly that Dallas was breaking, and had turned to Shorty for confirmation of the incredible progress that had been made.

Shorty had nodded his grudging agreement, but then looked at Dallas narrowly. 'There's more to you than meets the eye, Tex, and I'm willing to bet most of it ain't sunshine and roses.'

Dallas had been fending off slightly barbed and hostile remarks from Shorty for several days, seemingly unperturbed, and unfailingly polite and disciplined. For the first time his patience seemed to wear a little thin. 'You're right,' he proclaimed coldly. 'Most of it "ain't".'

'Anything we should know about?' Shorty asked softly. 'You know, like what might have shown up in an employment application if we had such a thing?'

'Shorty,' Mac said nervously, 'Dallas is——'

Dallas silenced him with a glance that said clearly he would fight his own battles. His eyes returned to Shorty's face, throwing diamond sparks of fire and ice. 'I don't think there's anything about me that effects the way I do my job,' he said dangerously, 'and as an employer that's all you're entitled to know. Did you have any particular questions?'

'No,' Shorty admitted, but there was a sly, smug light in his eyes, and Cory suspected that he had confirmed something that he wanted very badly to know. But what, she wondered?

Impatiently she threw off her covers, wrapped her housecoat around her and made her way through the darkened house to the kitchen. The bright light, and a steaming cup of cocoa helped to dispel the uneasiness she had felt in the darkness of her room, and she was beginning to think she was probably making something out of nothing.

The kitchen door squealed on its rusty hinges, and she looked up to see Dallas poised there, obviously tempted to turn and leave again. He was soaked to the skin, and she realised he'd probably been out walking in the pouring rain since after dinner. Had he been more disturbed by Shorty's prying than he let on?

'Do you want a cocoa?'

He hesitated, and then came in. 'Okay.'

She poured him cocoa, and then brought him a thick bath towel. He unselfconsciously stripped off his sodden shirt, towelled his head and chest vigorously, unaware that his golden, sinewy skin was wreaking havoc on Cory's senses.

'What are you doing up so late, Cory?' he asked, the towel looped around his neck, looking brilliantly white against the curling black hairs on his chest and his bronze skin.

'I couldn't sleep.' She paused. 'Dallas, what was Shorty getting at?'

He regarded her intently. 'Is that what kept you awake?' he asked softly.

'Sort of,' she admitted.

'Why?' he asked.

'I don't know. It seemed kind of sinister.'

Dallas laughed easily. 'You've been reading too many cloak and daggers, Cory.'

'Don't make fun of me, Dallas! Does he know something about you you'd rather he didn't know?'

Dallas regarded her thoughtfully. 'I don't think so.'

'There is something, isn't there?' she asked weakly.

His voice was even. 'There are some things in my life I'm not very proud of, yes.'

'Like what?' she asked fearfully.

'Thanks for the cocoa,' he said, pushing back his chair abruptly and rising. He reached for his shirt.

'Dallas——' Her voice, to her horror dissolved, and the tears sprang from behind her lashes. It all seemed suddenly too much—his indifference of the past days, and now this last gesture of shutting her out.

He stood very still, and then with a soft muttered oath, he dropped the shirt, crossed the room, gathered her in his arms and held her tightly against his naked broad chest.

He stroked her hair with unbelievable gentleness. 'Don't cry, Cory. I promise—I haven't deserted a wife and ten kids in Texas. I'm not running from the law. I haven't even robbed a corner store.'

She giggled shakily, and he lifted her chin. She found herself gazing into eyes dark with worry and tenderness.

'Dammit, Cory,' he said softly. 'Dammit.' Savagely, as though he were angry with himself for giving in, or with her for tempting him, he claimed her lips, bruising them ruthlessly, forcing them to part under the command of his.

And despite his savagery, she felt the joy building in her, and beating in an incredible tattoo. She returned his passion with all her pent-up intensity and hunger, melting into him, and feeling as though she were becoming a part of him.

His lips broke away from hers, though his embrace still locked her to him. His eyes lingered on her upturned face, as deeply and as captivatingly blue as she had ever seen them.

'It's late,' he said huskily, his arms falling away from her. She watched unsteadily as he moved away, picked up his shirt and headed for the door.

'Dallas, what about——?'

'Cory.' He stopped her. 'I make it a point never to worry about tomorrow. It's definitely going to come, and all my worrying or yours, isn't going to change what it holds.' The door creaked shut behind him.

She felt suddenly exhausted, contented and tumultuous all at once. Nothing was solved and nothing was resolved. And all her worrying wasn't going to change a thing. Wearily she climbed the steps to her room.

Were the barriers finally down? Cory wondered sleepily. Had that strangely savage and reluctant kiss meant he was finally willing to put the pain of the past—whatever that was—behind him? She wanted to believe it. She wanted desperately to believe that the intimacy that she had just experienced was more—much more—than an explosion of tension.

But the following morning, it seemed to Cory that she had foolishly overestimated the meaning of that kiss, and that Dallas had been intentionally cruel and unfeeling in bestowing it on her in the first place. She'd still been floating in its memory, when the phone had rung, bringing her harshly back to earth.

'Hello, Cory.' The voice was sugary sweet. 'Is that handsome man of mine around?'

'Shelly?' Cory responded with deliberate stupidity.

The voice grew cold. 'It's Nancy. I'd like to speak with Dallas.'

'He's at work,' Cory returned with equal frostiness.

She heard the other girl yawn. 'How can anybody function this early? Would you have him call me? It's about tonight.'

Drop dead, Cory said to herself. To Nancy she

replied with a restrained, 'I'll see that he gets your message.'

The fury boiled in her as she slammed down the receiver. How dare that man pretend that he cared about her, she thought, when he was making dates with Nancy Jacobsen? The circumstances surrounding that kiss didn't even cross her mind—only a fiery sense of betrayal, and deep anger with herself for having allowed her hopes to reach such impossible heights, only to be dashed.

'Who was that?' Tilda asked.

'Nancy *Jerk*ison,' Cory replied bitterly.

'Cory!' Tilda reprimanded. 'What did she want?'

'She wanted to talk to that handsome man of hers,' Cory mimicked disdainfully.

'Dallas?' Tilda asked, her voice heavy with unwanted understanding.

'Who else?' Cory snapped tersely. 'Don't look at me like that, Tilda. I couldn't care less who that arrogant, pompous ass goes out with.' With a proud toss of her head, she went out the door and headed in the direction of the barn.

She marched by where Dallas was saddling Raiser, quelling impatiently the dull ache that the sight of his rippling arm and shoulder muscles caused within her.

'Cory.'

She continued with her head high pretending, impossibly, not to have heard him.

'Cory!' Suddenly he was striding at her side.

'What do you want?' she asked irritably, stopping and glaring at him.

His eyes narrowed at her tone. 'I just wondered if you were feeling a little better this morning.' She avoided his probing gaze, keeping her eyes fixed steadfastly on the weathered side of the barn.

'I'm feeling just fine,' she responded coolly, and began to walk again.

'What the hell?' He grabbed her arm with a strength that whirled her and she faced him doggedly. 'What's the matter with you?' he asked quietly, his eyes sweeping her flushed face.

'Nothing!' she denied, jerking her arm away from him, and continuing with long, angry strides towards the barn.

'Cory,' his long stride brought him abreast of her easily. 'Tell me what happened.' It was not a request, but a command.

'Nothing happened!' she hissed. 'But get this straight, Dallas Hawthorne. I am not a part of your real or imagined caseload. If you want to play social worker, please dedicate yourself to Missy Henderson. She can use all the affection and sympathy you want to shower on her. And if you want to play Romeo, play with Nancy. She's more evenly matched with you in every way!'

'I don't know what you're talking about,' he insisted, meeting her eyes with growing anger of his own.

'Don't you?' she asked, stopping and facing him. 'Let me spell it out for you. I don't want you to kiss me—not ever again. And I don't want you to hold me as if I were some ridiculous child who needed the comfort of your big strong arms. I don't want to hear anymore of your two-bit philosophies on life. In other words, Dallas Hawthorne, I want nothing more to do with you— not ever! Is that clear enough for you?'

'That's pretty clear,' he replied through tight lips. He turned from her abruptly. 'See you around, Miss McConnel,' he called sardonically over his shoulder.

Tilda turned with surprise to the big man who

leaned against the doorframe, his arms folded across his powerful chest, and his face unreadable, except for the flinty sparks that flew from his eyes.

'What happened to Cory?' he demanded softly.

Tilda hastily hid her smile from him. 'It might have had something to do with that phone call,' she replied turning to the sink to hide the inner mirth that was starting to shake within her.

'What phone call?' Dallas asked quietly, suddenly dangerously close to Tilda's ear.

'Didn't Cory give you your message?' Tilda asked with feigned surprise.

'She gave me a message, all right, but I have a feeling it's not the one you're talking about.'

'Nancy called, and asked to speak to *her* man.'

Dallas stared at Tilda, and then sank into a kitchen chair, understanding dawning in his eyes. He sighed, studying his hands with troubled eyes. But to Tilda's grave disappointment, he got up silently and left without sharing his dilemma with her.

In the dream, they were still fighting and Dallas was shaking her ruthlessly. But slowly, Cory realised it wasn't entirely a dream, and pulled her eyes open.

Mac was bending over her, and something in his face made her sit up, suddenly wide awake and afraid.

'What is it?' she asked, the whiteness in his face filling her with terror.

'Tilda, Cory. Tilda's real sick. I've got to take her to the hospital.' He was shaking like a leaf in an autumn breeze.

'Maybe it's not that bad.' Quickly she threw back the covers and struggled into her housecoat. She flew down the hall to Tilda's room. She knew

instantly that it was 'that bad'. The usually stoic
Tilda was crying in pain, her hands firmly clasped
around her stomach. Cory felt sick now, as well as
afraid. Tilda had to get to a hospital and fast. The
nearest one was Calgary, and she knew that if she
tried to take the wheel through the city feeling as
frightened and shaken as she did she would
probably kill them all. She glanced at Mac, and
knew that he would be even worse.

'I'm going to get Dallas.' Despite Nancy, despite
the fact he'd ignored her all through lunch and
supper, and despite her anger with him, turning to
Dallas in an emergency seemed automatic, and she
could feel her panic subsiding.

Tilda nodded, grasping immediately the wisdom
of the decision, and Cory dashed barefoot out of
the house and across the cold frosty ground to the
bunkhouse.

She pounded frantically on the door, almost
collapsing with relief when the door was flung
open and Dallas stood before her, naked to the
waist in a hastily pulled on pair of jeans. The
slightly annoyed look vanished as his eyes swept
her face.

'What is it Cory?'

'Dallas, Tilda's really sick.'

Without waiting for further explanation, he
slid his bare feet into a pair of cowboy boots by
the door, and tugged a shirt off the hanger behind
it. He was pulling it over his broad shoulders even
as he was racing across the ground to the main
house.

'Have you ever had your appendix out?' he was
asking Tilda when Cory came in. He was crouched
beside the bed, and though he looked concerned,
Cory noted thankfully that his face reflected none
of her and Mac's panic.

Tilda shook her head, her tear-filled eyes pleading with him to do something. He smiled reassuringly at her, gently pulled back the covers, and scooped her up as if she was as light as Missy Henderson. 'Don't worry. We'll get you to a hospital and you'll be feeling better in no time.' He made his way quickly down the stairs, throwing an authoritative, 'Bring some blankets and a pillow,' at Cory.

He settled Tilda in the back of the station wagon, impatiently herded Mac and Cory into the front seat, and revved the engine.

Cory was crammed up against his big shoulder, and she watched with fascination as the speedometer jumped to a speed that far exceeded what she'd thought the wagon was capable of. But there was no doubting that Dallas was in control, and she felt exhilaratingly fearless sitting at his side.

At the same time as he expertly manoeuvered the car down the dark country lane, he grilled Tilda until he seemed satisfied that he'd heard all her symptoms. He turned his full concentration to the road, pushing the car to even greater speeds.

The trip flew by, dream-like. Where were the police, Cory kept wondering, once they hit the city? Dallas would slow down for red lights, look both ways, honk the horn and flash the lights, and then gun the car through them. His face remained as composed as if he were driving to a Sunday picnic.

Dallas, it occurred to her, was not fazed by crisis. He handled the car, and Tilda, and Mac, and herself with an almost professional calm. He had told Shelly that he was a born cowboy, and Cory had assumed he had never done anything else. Now she wasn't so certain. What, in a cowboy's experience, would prepare him to face a life-and-death emergency with such steel-nerved competence?

Cory somehow managed to give him directions to the nearest hospital, and congratulated herself almost giddily for being able to find it. They pulled up in the ambulance lane, and Dallas was out of the car in a flash, shouting instructions to the attendants who hurried back with a stretcher on wheels. Smiling reassurance at Tilda, he climbed into the back of the car and gently lifted her out.

Mac was at her side grasping her hand, and Cory followed behind as they wheeled her in. 'We've got to take her,' a nurse insisted to Mac, trying to pry his stubborn hand from Tilda's.

Dallas materialised at his side. Firmly, and yet with unmistakable gentleness he separated Mac's hand from Tilda's, at the same time as giving the nurse a run-down of the symptoms that Tilda had described to him in the car.

Then he led Mac and Cory down the hall to a cheerful waiting room, sat Mac down firmly, winked at Cory, and left again. When he returned a few minutes later he had finally done up the buttons of his shirt, and he carried two steaming cups of coffee. He folded Mac's hands carefully around one, handing the other to Cory, still totally unperturbed and still totally in control. Cory took a long sip, meeting Dallas' eyes as he sank down in the big arm chair across from her.

'You haven't always been a cowboy, have you, Dallas?'

His eyebrows lifted in surprise. 'What would make you think that?' he drawled softly.

She felt a little silly. 'I'm not sure. Just something about the way you're handling all this. You're so calm.'

'Please don't keep me in suspense,' he commented drily. 'What do you think I've done besides being a cowboy?'

She really wished she hadn't mentioned it at all. 'Driven an ambulance?' she ventured timidly. 'Or a race car?' she added with more enthusiasm.

Dallas chuckled, making her feel like an overly imaginative and amusing child. She glared at him, which only seemed to heighten his amusement.

'Well?' she demanded. She was a little tired of Dallas being so deliberately tight-lipped about his past, and not feeling at all inclined to let him get away with it this time.

'Well,' he returned seriously, 'I've never driven an ambulance or a race car.' He caught the determined glint in her eyes. 'But I have been forced to do some things I would rather not have done,' he conceded quietly.

At that moment, a young doctor came in and told them Tilda's appendix had almost burst. 'We'll be operating in a few minutes. There's nothing at all to worry about, though in another fifteen minutes there would have been a lot to worry about.'

'Dallas,' Mac said slowly, 'I think you saved her life. Cor and I—we couldn't drive like that. Thank you.'

Dallas nodded casually, then stretched long legs in front of him, and crossed his arms over his chest. Within moments his chin was resting on his chest and his breathing was deep and regular; the conversation of earlier irrevocably closed.

Cory's eyes roved around the room. And then back to him. He looked younger asleep, younger and strangely vulnerable. As if his face was incapable of the dry, mocking amusement that so often lurked there. Incapable of the icy anger she'd seen in it, and especially incapable of that mysterious hardness that crept into his features, turning them to stone.

Seeing him asleep, she felt overwhelmed with loving him. She would have liked to cross the room and run her fingers through his jet-black hair, and trace the proud curve of his high cheekbone with her small finger, and then cradle his sleeping head against her shoulder.

She sighed. She'd almost forgotten she was angry with him. Almost forgotten about Nancy. She looked hard at him. Dallas forced to do things he would rather not have done? She had trouble envisioning Dallas being forced to do anything he wasn't of a mind to do. What could have forced him? Necessity and hunger? And what would he have done? Washed dishes in a greasy spoon or waited on tables? The very thought struck Cory as being ludicrous, and certainly wouldn't account in any way for his steadying calm.

Where have you been, Dallas? she questioned the sleeping face. What have you done to make you the man you are? And why won't you let me in? Why won't you ever let me get close to you?

It was quite a while later when the doctor returned and told them that the operation had gone well, and suggested they all go home. In all that time, Cory had remained lost in thought, her eyes fastened on Dallas' face.

She rose slowly, hesitated, and then gave Dallas a gentle shake. He awakened, looked surprised to see her, and then smiled boyishly, as if seeing her first thing when he woke up agreed with him.

'Tilda's fine. We can go home.' But for a moment her hand stayed pressed gently against his shoulder, their eyes locked in silent and searching wonder. Dallas stretched, and she snatched her hand away, the spell broken.

Though neither she nor Mac had been able to sleep in the hospital waiting room, they had no sooner left the last of the bright city lights behind them, when both drifted off.

'Cory, we're home,' Mac said, nudging her none too gently. 'Wake up.'

Cory blinked at him, smiled groggily, and snuggled deeper into the arm that was around her shoulders. 'I'm okay here,' she mumbled contentedly, slipping quickly back into sleep.

'I've got her,' Dallas told Mac, cradling her easily in his muscular arms.

'Must get tired of hauling people around,' Mac muttered, leading the way into the house and waving a tired hand at Cory's bedroom door. He stumbled down the hall to his own room.

Dallas deposited Cory gently on her bed. She stirred and mumbled something unintelligible, but slept on. He towered over her tiny form, as if mesmerised by her sleeping face. His gaze, for once unguarded, once again looked young, in a strange mixture of longing and agony.

'If only you knew, Cory,' he whispered, 'if only you knew.'

CHAPTER SIX

CORY awoke the next morning feeling an odd sensation of elation, and at first she couldn't place its source. And then she remembered the look in Dallas' eyes when she'd woken him at the hospital last night. She remembered that Tilda was all right. She realised she was in her own bed and also knew how she must have got here. It was a brand new day, and her stomach had an expectant flutter in it—as though something exciting was going to happen to her.

The feeling lasted exactly half an hour. Then she found Mac's note. It stated simply that he'd gone back to Calgary to be with Tilda and that she would have to look after things. The full impact of 'looking after things' hit Cory like an unexpected blow to the solar plexus. Cook? Clean? She would have sat down and wailed with frustration, except that she realised she didn't have time for that tiny self-indulgence. The men would be in for lunch soon.

She cringed at the thought of having to put her domestic failings on display. Cameron would tease, Shorty would complain, and Dutch would be brave. She knew she could handle these reactions with ease. It was Dallas' she was worried about. No doubt, he would write her off as a complete loss in yet one more area that required a little feminine know-how.

Quickly she banished these self-doubts, deciding firmly that she would show them all. Now, where to begin? she wondered, and opened a cupboard. The shelves were lined with canned goods, and she smiled, taking out several cans of beans.

'See, Tilda,' she muttered, 'there isn't much to this cooking stuff.' The beans were bubbling briskly on the stove when the men came in, and Cory felt exceedingly competent. She poured the beans into a large serving crock, noting with a little less confidence that they seemed to have melted into an indistinguishable mush. They'd taste fine, she assured herself. Mac, on his tales of long cattle drives, always said the only thing a trail cook couldn't ruin was beans.

She cut off some chunks of Tilda's homemade bread, squashing it miserably as she did so. Who would have thought, she wondered with annoyance, that cutting bread required technique? Undaunted, she placed the bread on the table and sat down.

She took one bite of her meal, and her worst fears were confirmed. The 'unruinable' beans were dreadful. She sighed unhappily, caught herself, and glared at each man defiantly, daring them to comment. Though she treated Dallas to the same look as the rest of them, she couldn't help but wonder if he was disappointed in her. When he winked good-naturedly, she decided blackly that he didn't have any expectations of her in the first place.

She'd show them, she thought ferociously. After all, she hadn't had much time to prepare this lunch. But for supper she'd prepare something absolutely dazzling. She could almost picture how Dallas' eyes would rest on her with a new and admiring light in them. She was so lost in her plans that she hardly noticed the men filing quietly out of the kitchen, their deserted plates hardly touched.

Was the way to a man's heart really through his stomach? Roast beef, just the way Tilda made it, might be a good test of that old adage. The fact that she didn't have a clue how Tilda made it didn't deter her in the least.

She took a joint of beef out of the freezer, stared at it blankly, and then with a merry shrug, stripped the paper off it, filled a huge pot with water, threw the roast in, and turned the burner on high. Nothing to it, she congratulated herself, envisioning Dallas carving a tender brown roast. By the time the phone rang, potatoes and carrots had joined the roast, and Cory was totally absorbed in acting out the dinner inside her head. Oddly enough, Dutch, Cameron, and Shorty weren't even there anymore, and there were candles and a bottle of sparkling champagne on the table. With a start she drew herself back to reality and answered the phone.

'How's it going, Cory?' Mac asked uninterestedly.

'Great!' she responded enthusiastically.

'Good. Look Cory, Tilda's fine, but they still want to keep her here for awhile. Probably about a week.'

'A week?' Cory wailed, and then quickly collected herself. The most important thing was that Tilda was all right. 'Okay.'

'She's already insisting she's ready to go home, stubborn old mule. I'm going to get a room near the hospital and stay here. If Tilda got too lonely, she'd probably just pack her bag and walk home.'

Cory smiled. 'I think you're right, Dad. I'll miss you though. Both of you.'

'Will you be all right? Tilda's pretty worried about you being able to manage.'

'Tell her not to worry,' Cory assured him, her eyes widening at the ugly grey foam bubbling out of the pot and dropping with angry hisses on to the red hot burner. She scowled. This definitely wasn't in the script.

'Tilda wants to know what you had for lunch,' Mac asked dubiously.

'Beans,' Cory replied, 'and roast for supper.' Maybe, she added to herself. 'Dad, I really have to go.' She hung up without waiting for him to say goodbye, and rushed over to the stove to turn the burner down. 'Yuck,' she said, scrunching up her pert nose at the gurgling mess in the burner well. However, calamity seemed to have been averted, and she allowed herself to become optimistic all over again that her supper was going to unfold exactly according to plan.

The afternoon flew by, and Dutch was standing sniffing at the door before she knew it. 'What's for supper?' he asked cautiously.

'Roast beef,' she answered a trifle triumphantly. She shoved a handful of plates at him. 'Set the table,' she ordered crisply.

Dutch sniffed indignantly but complied.

Cory lifted the roast out of the brew and laid it on a platter, aware suddenly of Dallas in the doorway. Her visions of candles and wine had already disappeared, and now her vision of a tender, brown roast went the same way. The grey mass looked like a rubber ball, she admitted with dismay, struggling to keep her optimism of earlier alive.

'Staying for dinner, Cameron?' she called to him, as he scrubbed his hands at the sink.

She missed his eyes widening at the hunk of meat sitting on the platter. 'No thanks,' he replied hastily, turning like a frightened animal and skulking past Dallas and Shorty out the door.

Cory was already peering back into her pot. The potato she tried to snare as it floated by her fork, crumbled at her touch. Sighing, she drained the water into a large gravy boat, and then dumped the slightly mashed potatoes and carrots into a bowl. Colourful, she told herself, with a certain degree of pride.

She was too busy to notice the mounting horror on Dutch and Shorty's faces as she assembled each dish on the table. Dutch scrutinised the watery contents of the gravy boat.

'What is this stuff?' he asked suspiciously when Cory took her place.

Cory scowled at him. 'Gravy,' she retorted, her tone making it quite clear that she wouldn't tolerate anymore imbecilic questions. She asked Dallas shyly to carve, and the last of the happy light faded in her eyes as he wrestled with the rubbery meat. This dinner was not turning out at all like her pleasant daydreams of this afternoon—in fact, it was more comparable to a nightmare.

She realised that all eyes were on her and she bravely sampled the roast. Chewy, she conceded, and not exactly tasty, but certainly edible. She smiled at her audience, and watched as they sampled their own plates.

Maybe Shorty and Dutch just weren't hungry, she told herself weakly, watching the dainty, cautious manner in which they were approaching their food. She shot Dallas a look, and noticed with relief that he was eating with his usual robust appetite. But then she noticed that Dutch and Shorty were also watching him, not even trying to hide their astonishment.

Slowly Dallas realised that he was the centre of attention, and set down his fork. 'What?' he asked quietly.

'You got a stomach lined with cast iron?' Dutch asked undiplomatically.

Dallas glanced at Cory's flushing face, and resumed eating. 'It's not all that bad,' he commented easily, but Cory heard only the implied it wasn't all that good either.

Stiffly she finished her dinner, and got up from the table. She pretended not to notice the creaking of the garbage lid as soon as her back was turned.

'When's Tilda going to be home?' Shorty asked bluntly, depositing his plate at her elbow.

'A week,' Cory replied miserably. The silence that greeted that announcement reflected her misery. Cory allowed her shoulders to slump as she heard the kitchen empty.

'Want a hand with the dishes?' Dallas asked softly.

She squared her shoulders again. 'No.'

'Cory.'

'What?' she asked, a bit of a shrill note in her voice.

'It doesn't matter, you know.'

She whirled and stared at him. He couldn't possibly know how hard she had tried to impress him?

'What doesn't matter?' she asked weakly, hoping she had misunderstood him, praying that she wasn't so transparent.

But he confirmed her worst fears. 'It doesn't matter if you can't cook.'

She flushed, and yet her heart began to beat painfully and hopefully within her breast at the tenderness in his expression. Something in the way he had said that made it sound so personal— almost as if he'd added 'I'd have you anyway'.

'Dallas,' she whispered, the dishes and even the dinner forgotten. He hesitated, his eyes on her slightly parted and inviting lips, and she knew that he was a breath away from crossing the room and gathering her in his arms.

He took a swift step towards her, then stopped abruptly, shaking his head ever so slightly as if to clear a vision both disturbing and enticing. His eyes became suddenly sardonic.

'See you tomorrow.' He whirled, and left the room, leaving her standing alone, astonished and feeling empty and somehow cheated. Had she been mistaken? Had it been pity in those eyes, and not tenderness? Did she love him with such desperation that she was led to imagine, at the least little sign, that he loved her back?

She watched him stroll beneath the kitchen window, and hop in his truck. He was going to see Nancy, she deduced blackly. She took a dripping plate out of the sink, regarded it thoughtfully, and then threw it with all her strength against the wall.

She made pancakes the following morning, this time not even giving a damn whether they turned out or not. In fact, she felt a certain amount of grim satisfaction when Dallas cut into his stack, and gluey strings extended from his plate to his fork. Grimacing but stoic, he put the first bite in his mouth.

Dutch sighed and laid down his fork. 'A man's got limits, Dallas. I can't eat raw pancakes—not even to show Cory how much I appreciate her effort.'

So, Cory thought bitterly, it had been pity. Dallas felt so sorry for her that he'd asked everyone to pretend they liked her cooking. 'Don't eat them. I'll make some toast.'

The men ate in silence, and Cory studied the floor. She was relieved when they got up to leave, and she cleared the breakfast dishes methodically, and surveyed the mess in the kitchen with heaviness.

'Laundry's by the door here,' Dutch remarked casually.

'Laundry!' Cory whirled, and for the first time saw the large canvas bags, each neatly labelled with a name. 'Tilda does your laundry?' she asked weakly.

'Yeah,' Dutch confirmed apologetically. 'Look, maybe it can wait till she gets back, Cory.'

Cory shook her head wearily. The last thing she wanted was for Tilda to come home to mountains of dirty laundry. 'I'll do it.' She closed her eyes. She wasn't going to admit she didn't know how to do laundry with Dallas still here. She didn't want anymore of his pity. 'Would you guys please leave? I'd like to scream in private.'

Dutch chuckled with understanding. 'Don't worry, Cory. You'll catch on.'

'By the way, Cory,' Dallas commented casually, 'it might be a good idea to figure out what you're going to have for supper.'

'Supper?' she glared at him. 'It's six-thirty in the morning.'

'Which leaves you enough time to get something out of the freezer and thawed for supper,' Dallas countered drily.

'Get out,' Cory hissed softly, striving for control. 'All of you get out of this kitchen right now!'

They didn't need to be asked again. It was only after they'd left that she saw the cookbook that had been left unobtrusively on the table. She knew who would have left it and, without wanting to be, she was drawn to it.

Perhaps there would be something in it—an inscription or some notes, that would tell her something about Dallas and about the history he managed to be so elusive about. But the page that might have held an inscription had been torn out, and the rest, though well thumbed, told her nothing. She wondered briefly about that missing page. Had it held some tender message that was painful to him? But he'd kept the book—unwilling or unable to dismiss the memory of the giver entirely? Maybe he just liked the recipes, she thought firmly, putting the book down, and glaring at the laundry.

She decided to practise on Dutch's, since it would be less mortifying to ruin his clothes than Dallas'. She dragged the bag into the small laundry room off the kitchen, and dumped the contents unceremoniously into the washer. She couldn't find the laundry soap, so she added a generous amount of dish soap, turned on the washer, and retired into the living room with the cookbook.

Cory was astounded by the number of easy recipes and marked interesting page numbers in a notebook beside her. 'That should do for about a week,' she finally decided, surveying her long list of page numbers. She slammed the book shut and went to check on the laundry.

She stood in the kitchen door, staring dumbly at the mountains of white foam that had taken over the kitchen. The washer was still burping out white clouds with indifferent ease. Slowly, the reality of the situation dawned on her, and with growing despair she waded through the waist-high suds, sat down on the only chair she could find and rested her elbows on the table. She stared bleakly at the billowing clouds of bubbles, and then gave in completely to self-pity.

'I can't do this,' she wailed out loud. 'I just can't do this.' For some reason, Tilda's question of several weeks ago—about what kind of man would ever marry her—was suddenly remembered and it fuelled her self-pity. She began to weep helplessly.

She didn't hear the back door open, but she did hear the soft chuckle that quickly dissolved into deep and robust laughter. She looked up sharply, trying desperately to control her tears, but they wouldn't stop—in fact, they were coming harder now, as Dallas held his sides and rocked with uncontrollable mirth. There were tears in his own eyes when he finally struggled to meet her gaze.

'I'm sorry,' he gasped apologetically, not missing her distressed expression. He waded through the frothing white, the force of his powerful stride engulfing him in a blizzard of floating, feathery blobs.

Suddenly, Cory began to laugh, too. She tried to tell herself sternly that it wasn't at all funny, but her natural sense of humour won out. Dallas joined her at the table and they laughed until the tears coursed down their faces. And for a long time after the laughter had died they sat gazing at each other, and relishing in the fond bond of affection that had been created by the shared joke.

She began to feel the familiar current of electricity coming alive between them, and her eyes longed for and invited his kiss. But once again, he hesitated, and then backed away from that invitation.

'I'll go get some help,' he volunteered quickly, getting up suddenly as though he no longer trusted himself to be alone with her. He returned shortly with the hands, once again composed and casual.

And when his eyes met hers through the ensuing blizzard, they were laughing and nothing more. And though he playfully buried her in suds, and flicked light snowballs at her, he seemed vaguely and disturbingly withdrawn.

Cameron brought in his camera and took pictures of it all, and Cory joined the merriment, laughing and shouting as much as the rest of them, though part of her, too, withdrew, as she tried to analyse and understand if and why Dallas was fighting his feelings for her.

Later, she watched from the kitchen window as the soaking wet ranch-hands crossed to the bunkhouse. Her eyes fastened on Dallas, his muscular form tantalisingly outlined beneath his sodden clothes. She sighed with heart-felt longing, and agony.

Who else could have turned such a disaster into a playful adventure? Who else could have taken the heart of a young girl and turned it into that of a woman? Who else could make her feel so vibrantly and totally alive? She knew, bleakly, that the answer to all those questions was no one else. And she knew just as bleakly, that he sensed she was holding her heart out to him like a gentle gift, and that he chose to walk away. She wondered sadly if she was doomed to dream forever of a love that was never to be.

'Why, Dallas?' she whispered. 'Why?'

'Tell me, Dallas,' Shorty said while they were sipping coffee after Cory's first really successful meal, 'you must have been about the right age to get mixed up in that Vietnam stuff, you being an American and all.'

Dallas seemed to freeze, his gaze narrow and hard on Shorty's face. 'Are you asking if I'm in Canada because I dodged the draft?' His voice was soft—dangerously soft.

'Hell, no,' Shorty denied, but something in his tone warned Cory this was really a continuation of what he'd started the other night. What was he digging for? 'Just curious. Were you over there?'

'I was there,' Dallas bit out tersely, his eyes dark with wariness and danger.

Cory recognised that the hard and mysterious part of Dallas was once again unsheathed, but this time there was a subtle difference. She suspected that Shorty had inadvertently touched its core, and that the answer to the despairing 'why' she had asked that afternoon was, in a way she couldn't quite fathom, related to this experience.

No wonder, she thought abstractedly, Dallas remained so calm in a situation she had called an emergency. After some of the things he must have seen and done and experienced in combat, a case of appendicitis must have seemed mild stuff to him.

Shorty either ignored or missed the warning note that should have cleared him off the subject of Vietnam. 'Get any gooks?' he asked with appalling eagerness.

'If I did,' Dallas' voice had gone low with tension and contempt, 'it's not something I'm proud of.'

The statement sent a chill through Cory. Dallas had killed people, she thought. What else would have caused that flash of intense and unbearable pain in his midnight eyes? She felt suddenly ill.

Dallas, who had held Missy with such gentle arms, had held a rifle with those same arms. Dallas, whose strong arms had strained to give the gift of life to a tiny, helpless calf, had taken aim and squeezed the trigger. Dallas, who had promised her passion under the glowing stars and the porch light had——

She stopped. Finally, she understood the frightening coldness in him. But looking into his eyes she had the uneasy feeling that there was something more to this story.

'Weren't you a hero, or anything?' Shorty asked with whining disappointment.

'No,' Dallas replied sharply, his eyes snapping with carefully controlled fury. 'No,' he repeated, more quietly. 'I wasn't a hero.'

'Drop it, Shorty,' Dutch commanded gruffly, his eyes full of uncharacteristic anger.

'Sure,' Shorty conceded easily, but in the back of her mind Cory registered that he seemed rather satisfied about something. But her mind was racing too tumultuously to dwell on it.

She'd pushed Dallas the other night at the hospital. And all he'd said was that he'd been forced to do some things he would rather not have done. She'd thought of washing dishes, for cripes sake!

And that other night, when he'd assured her that he hadn't deserted a wife, or robbed a store, he'd left the worst part unsaid. Had he been protecting her? Had he seen how narrow and sheltered her life was, that doing dishes was about the most unpleasant thing she could think of?

Or was he protecting himself from things too painful to be remembered, to be shared?

Dallas stood up, and Cory had never seen a man look so dangerous. His face was icily impassive, but his eyes held killing contempt, and his tension showed in the flickering muscle in his jaw, and the pulse beating rapidly in the hollow of his throat. Shorty shrank from his gaze, taking sudden interest in his coffee.

Dallas turned, anger static in the air around him, and left. Without hesitation Cory scrambled from her chair and followed him out into the night.

'Dallas,' she called softly, coming up behind him, and touching his arm.

He turned and looked at her impatiently, and though his anger filled her with pain, it didn't frighten her. Suddenly he sighed, the tension easing out of his coiled muscles.

'Leave me alone, Cory,' he said wearily. 'Just leave me alone.'

He'd shut her out again—unwilling or unable to accept the sympathy and understanding she sensed he needed desperately. Unwilling or unable to accept the only cure she knew for an aching, bruised and world-weary heart—love.

For a moment she stood stock still, studying his face. Had there been even the smallest chink in that cold armour, even the remotest pleading in his eyes, she would have wrapped her arms around him and waited for the storm that lived within him to unleash itself.

But his face was unmarred by human emotion—arrogant in the silver paint of the moonlight.

'Leave me alone, Cory,' he repeated, this time more harshly.

Sadly, she turned away from him, knowing he had pushed her away once too often.

She realised that she wouldn't be able to stop loving him, but she had to somehow make herself less open to him, so that his indifference and his stunning coldness could not leave her feeling so devastated.

He looked tired the following morning, and despite her resolve, she felt rather shaken. With supreme effort she turned away from his haggard face, quelling the longing to comfort him. He had made it amply clear that he didn't want any comfort, and to offer it would only leave her open to being hurt again.

She immersed herself in the business of looking after the house and doing the cooking, a little amazed by how all-encompassing that job was, and even more amazed by her growing competence at it.

The book Dallas had provided her with was definitely geared to getting polished results from beginners, and after her initial panic subsided, she found she remembered helpful little tips from her home economics class, and from having helped Tilda now and then.

She wouldn't have ever admitted to liking cooking, but she did begin to feel confident enough to try a few more complicated recipes, and couldn't even pretend to hide her delight when every crumb of a chocolate cake she'd baked, disappeared at one sitting. Besides, the cooking and cleaning absorbed her attention, and drained her energy. She couldn't very well be up to her elbows in flour, following directions, and mooning about Dallas at the same time. In fact, she was rather pleased with the efficient, competent and calm exterior she managed to present. No one was ever going to suspect how her heart still ached when he walked into the room, or how it raced when his elbow brushed hers as he deposited his dishes in the sink.

She thought he tried a few times to penetrate the barrier that she had erected around herself, but reminded herself grimly that she was quite capable of imagining things where he was concerned. And one thing she wasn't imagining was that he left the ranch every night for a few hours after dinner. She had not the slightest doubt where he went and who he saw, and her resolve deepened until her heart felt like it was sheathed in thick layers of ice.

Tilda came home, and the men applauded her first meal with a delighted enthusiasm that Cory reluctantly endorsed.

At the end of that meal, Dallas rocked back his chair and eyed Cory, the unmistakable mischief in his expression making Cory immediately wary.

'I think,' he said to the room in general, though his eyes never left her, 'that because Cory made such an admirable effort last week, she deserves a night on the town. I intend to give it to her—tomorrow night.' He was smiling pleasantly, but his eyes held challenge. 'I'm going to take you out to dinner.'

'That isn't necessary,' Cory responded swiftly and coldly. Downright dangerous, she added to herself, scowling at Dallas. It had been a fairly simple matter to keep those carefully constructed barriers intact when there were always people around, and a million things to busy herself doing. But being alone with him? What was he trying to prove?

'Cor, it's a wonderful idea!' Mac insisted. 'You really deserve it. You're going and that's an order from the boss—me.'

'I second that,' Tilda joined in warmly. 'What a lovely idea, Dallas.'

You cunning devil, Cory thought meeting his gaze haughtily, but knowing she was trapped. To refuse would be to invite more argument from Tilda and Mac, and she knew them both well enough to know they wouldn't give up until she gave in. And Dallas knew it, too, she thought. He'd just sit back and enjoy himself as they won his battle for him. She gave him a cold, curt nod.

'Be ready at seven,' he commanded casually, and left the table.

She glared at his broad back with frustration. Why, she wondered wearily, wouldn't he just leave her alone? Wouldn't it be just the same old merry-go-round? Wouldn't he just pull her close, only to push her away again?

She wondered with a heartfelt sigh if he hated her. Why else would he torture her over and over again?

CHAPTER SEVEN

She wore her dress from Marcelle's, telling herself that it was because she had no idea where he was taking her, and certainly not because she wanted him to find her attractive. But she knew, as she regarded herself in the mirror, that her blazing cheeks denied the coldness that she wanted Dallas to believe she felt.

He was waiting in the living room in a grey suit, the cut and expense of which rivalled the blue one he had worn to the social. He looked, she admitted with a touch of well-concealed awe, fabulously handsome and unnervingly worldly.

He held open the truck door for her, and she slid by him, cold-faced.

'Why are you doing this?' she asked stiffly, her eyes straight ahead.

He hesitated. 'I behaved badly the other night, Cory. I needed to be alone and I was angry. I didn't mean to be harsh with you, and I didn't mean to hurt your feelings.'

'You didn't need to bring me for dinner to tell me that. Besides, you're quite overestimating my reaction.'

'Really?' he queried softly. 'I've been trying for a week to tell you exactly that. I could have sworn you were giving me the cold-shoulder.'

'I was just busy,' she said uncomfortably and unconvincingly. 'Where are we going?' she asked, eager to change the subject.

'A place in Calgary.'

'Calgary? Dallas, there are places to eat closer than Calgary.'

'But not like this one. I think you'll like it.'

She gave him a sideways glance to see if he was feeling the same excruciating tension that she was. He looked as relaxed as though he was taking his kid sister to the movies she noted with aggravation.

'I notice you're not wearing an engagement ring.' His face was composed, and his tone strictly conversational.

'I told Timmy no,' she said softly. She steeled herself to respond to any further probing with indifference, but Dallas only smiled at her with such warmth that her heart cartwheeled crazily against her ribcage.

'I came across the graveyard in the grove behind your house today,' he said after a while. 'Your mother's?'

The question caught her off guard again. He was so damned complex! How could a man capable of such hardness as Dallas also be so gentle?

'Yes,' she replied, still striving to be cold.

'I'm sorry, it must have been very hard on you.'

'I was only six.' She hesitated, knowing she could leave it at that, but somehow she didn't want to. 'At first I didn't know what dead meant. But then Dad sort of crumpled, and I realised how terrible it was—that neither of us were ever going to see her again

'I can still see her face, the way she looked when she tucked me in at night, the smell of her perfume clinging to my pyjamas. I remember how safe and warm and secure I always felt. Tilda has always been wonderful, but it wasn't the same. I guess I'm probably such a tomboy because I wouldn't let Dad out of my sight for years after that—always riding up in front of him, or right beside him, trailing him around the ranch like a little lost pup. I had this funny idea that he would have liked a boy better, and I did my darndest to accomodate him, despite all Tilda's efforts to make a little lady out of me.'

Dallas chuckled. 'Nothing against Tilda, but you're a delightful failure.'

Cory stared awkwardly at her hands. Damn this man! Sometimes he could make it sound so much like he liked her—really liked her, just as she was, complete with all her tomboy rough edges. She couldn't bear to dwell on the thought, and was eager to remove the focus from herself.

'What about your family, Dallas?'

'My parents are dead,' he said and she heard iciness that rivalled that which had been in his voice the other night when he was reminded of Vietnam. She had a feeling that this, too, was part of his bitterness and mystery, and she wanted desperately to draw him out about it. At the same time she wasn't eager to be rebuked as she had been the other night when she had tried to comfort him.

'I'm sorry,' she finally offered, feeling she should say more, but not knowing what to say.

'Don't be,' he shrugged indifferently. 'It was a long time ago.'

Her mother's death had been a long time ago, too, she thought puzzled, and it still hurt and she was still sorry. She looked thoughtfully at his strong profile. He glanced back at her, and his eyes held unmistakable warning that the subject was off limits.

'How come,' she asked flippantly, anxious to change the subject, 'you own suits like that? They hardly seem appropriate for a man in your line of work.' The comment was calculated to put him on edge—to strengthen her carefully constructed barrier, a barrier that was becoming rapidly threatened just by his nearness.

But he only laughed softly. 'It's my conceit,' he teased. 'I just love to look good and impress people—especially pretty girls.'

'You don't have to wear a suit to look good,' Cory blurted out, and then could have happily stuffed her fist in her mouth for having let it slip out. 'What I mean is——'

'Don't retract,' he interrupted easily. 'That's a nice way to start a truce.'

'A temporary truce,' she corrected him frigidly.

'Yes,' he agreed softly, 'a temporary truce.'

Suddenly, inexplicably, she didn't want to hurt him anymore. Or be angry with him. She wanted to forget this evening was nothing more to him than a gesture—an apology, and a token of appreciation. Maybe it wouldn't hurt to pretend, just this once, that this handsome Texan was her date, that he was here because he liked her, or maybe even loved her a bit. Maybe that wouldn't hurt at all, she thought, sliding him a cautious look from under the veil of her eyelashes, and allowing her heart a tiny twinge of yearning.

He drove through the hectic downtown traffic with ease, and Cory gasped with pleasure and dismay when he pulled up in front of the Calgary Inn, and the red-jacketed doorman came out and opened her door for her.

'Dallas.' She sent him a frantic glance, but he was already out of his door and handing the keys to the doorman. He came around the truck, and took her arm firmly.

'Dallas, we can't go in here. It's too——'

'Hush,' he ordered sternly, leading her through the luxurious lobby to the oak doors of the restaurant. A smiling, impeccably groomed *maître d'* greeted them. 'Mr Hawthorne, please follow me. Your table is ready.'

'Does he know you?' Cory whispered, watching Dallas wide-eyed.

'We must be the only seven-thirty reservation,' Dallas replied smoothly.

Of course, she thought. The *maître d'* of the Owl's Nest wouldn't know a cowhand by name. The exquisite décor required all her attention. She had seen restaurants this plush, this subtly romantic before—but only in the movies. The *maître d'* was holding back a chair for her and she sank into it, unable to take her eyes off the magnificent linen and sparkling china.

She fingered the silver with awe, and then started. 'Dallas,' her eyes met his fearfully, 'there must be ten forks here.' She felt awkward and suddenly horribly out of place. 'I don't know how to use them all,' she murmured self-consciously.

'Relax, Cory.' He reached reassuringly across the table and gave her hand a gentle squeeze. 'Just start from the outside and work in. Everything will fall into place.'

Was he laughing at her ignorance, she wondered with an inward cringe? She pulled her hand away and opened the leather-bound menu, regarding it steadfastly so that she wouldn't have to look at him.

She was determined to order the cheapest item on the menu. She wasn't altogether sure that Dallas knew what a place like this cost, even if he did seem so terribly at ease in the rich surroundings. She had no doubt that Dallas would seem terribly at ease no matter where he was, though she preferred not to test her theory in the kitchen of this establishment, facing a mountain of dishes.

'Dallas,' she stammered, 'there's something wrong with this menu. It doesn't have any prices on it.'

'The menu's fine, Cory,' he assured her with quiet patience. 'It's supposed to be like that.'

'Oh,' Cory murmured stupidly, not daring to ask him why, even though she wanted to know. At least his eyes had been kind, and not tinged with their usual measure of mocking laughter.

The waiter, despite his stiff black tuxedo and formal manners, had a relaxed smile and friendly eyes that made Cory feel slightly more at ease. She relaxed a little.

And then a little more after swallowing one sherry, and sipping a second one.

'Have you ever had Châteaubriand?' Dallas asked. Cory shook her head, and agreed quickly and with relief when Dallas suggested they try it.

'Tell me about Texas,' she insisted, made braver for the sherry.

'What would you like to know?'

'Tell me about the ranch you grew up on,' she said without hesitation.

He laughed. 'You're a different sort of girl, Cory. Most women would ask about the climate, and the beaches, and the shopping and night life in Dallas and Houston.'

'I'm not interested in those things,' Cory replied, feeling slightly inadequate.

'I know,' he said thoughtfully, as if he liked the fact. An unwilling thrill danced through her.

Dallas told her about the ranch. About its size, the amount of stock, the breeding programmes they'd used on the Hereford and quarter-horse stock. Cory was awed by the numbers he was talking. She'd heard things were big in Texas, but she hadn't been prepared for how big. The Flying M seemed like a hobby farm in comparison.

'Dallas, your family didn't own it, did they?' she asked in a small, rather awe-stricken voice.

'I'm afraid so,' he said with wry amusement, sensing her awe.

'You were rich!' she blurted out, understanding almost unwillingly why he was so at home in these surroundings.

'Filthy,' he agreed amiably. 'The ranch was only part of it. My father was an oilman. He called the ranch his hobby, which is rather amusing since he wouldn't have known one end of a horse from the other. It was actually a tax shelter.

'But I was born there, to the sound of bawling cattle, and I could ride before I could walk. My dad travelled a lot when I was a kid, and I kind of latched on to the ranch hands. By the time I was fifteen, I knew all the tricks it had taken six men their lifetimes to learn.

'I lived and breathed ranching—open skies, the feel of a good horse underneath me, campfires on clear nights, the smell of a brand against hide. To me—then and now—it was those things that made a man rich, not how much money he had in the bank.'

He had touched Cory's soul with his quiet description, giving words to some of the things she, too, loved about ranching. She suddenly didn't feel intimidated by the wealth he'd discussed, or by her rich surroundings. Because he was right. Open skies and fresh air and a good horse were what made you rich, inside if not outside, and she was wealthy, too—at least for a few more weeks.

'Why did you leave, Dallas? If you loved it so much?'

He shrugged. 'My dad and I had some differences of opinion.' His tone had once again become chilly and his eyes once again held warning. He didn't mention what had happened to the ranch after his parents had died. Had he been cut out of the will? Did that explain the bitterness that crept into his voice when he talked about them?

'What did you do?'

'I got involved in rodeo. My career was interrupted by being drafted,' a barely perceptible shadow clouded his dark eyes, 'and then I went back to rodeo, and what I'm doing now.'

'Do you still rodeo, Dallas?'

'I don't much anymore.' He grinned. 'The broken bones seem to hurt more, and take longer to heal than they used to.'

Cory hesitated. 'Haven't you ever wanted to settle down, Dallas? Haven't you ever wanted to have a place to call home? Don't you have dreams?' She blushed. 'I mean surely you can't——'

'Drift forever?' he finished for her, smiling. 'No,' he said softly, 'I think my drifting days are about over.' His eyes held hers with incredible intensity, as if she had something to do with that decision. The last of her resolve crumbled, and the horrible little hope began to pound in her heart again.

'And I do have a dream. Raiser is the beginning of it. I want to breed and train the finest working cattle horses in the world.'

'That's pretty ambitious, Dallas,' she said with a smile.

'Maybe. Now, what about you, Cory? Is there something you lie awake nights dreaming about?'

She blushed wildly, not, of course, being able to tell him the truth. 'I guess I'm a lot like you,

Dallas,' she finally said, collecting herself. 'I was born on the Flying M, and ranching is in my blood. Until a couple of weeks ago, I don't even think I had a dream—I was already living it. But now, I guess my dream is to have a place like the Flying M again someday. It's probably a silly dream for me, because I can't see how it would ever happen. But I guess dreams are allowed to be silly, aren't they?'

He didn't answer. 'No dreams of a husband and a family, Cory? It seems to me most girls want things like that.'

'I'm not most girls,' she whispered evasively, dropping her eyes from the ones that burned with amusement, and something she couldn't quite interpret.

'No, you're not,' he agreed softly. She realised suddenly that they had finished dinner, and that she hadn't even tasted it.

Warm piano notes were beginning to float through the room, and Cory sought their source. A young man, in elegant white tails, was sitting at the other end of the room playing a grand piano. She noticed the dance floor for the first time.

Dallas ordered Spanish coffee for them both, and she sipped hers with pleasure. When she was done, he held out his hand to her, and she quickly accepted, and was led to the dance floor.

Dancing with Dallas, she thought happily, was like floating through a fairytale. His arms were so strong and sure around her that she didn't even have to think about what to do. Her head nestled comfortably on the firm expanse of his chest, so close to his heart that she could hear its steady beating. His scent enveloped her, clean and masculine and comforting.

She knew, a little guiltily, that she was lying

when she brushed off his comment about the high colour blossoming in her cheeks as being the fault of too much wine. Her senses were wonderfully and exquisitely drunk, but the champagne they'd had with dinner had not been nearly as heady as was the closeness of him; the subtle pressure of his hard, muscular body against hers.

She could hardly believe it when he announced, she sensed reluctantly, that it was time for them to go. Somehow the night had melted into midnight without her being aware of the passage of time.

When he stopped the truck in the yard, he turned and looked at her with eyes that were dark and unreadable, then motioned her to move over beside him. Her desperate fight to keep her distance had ended over dinner, and she slid over to him, telling herself it had been too wonderful an evening to end with an aloof and impersonal good night. He gathered her in his arms, and held her close, softly stroking her glossy hair. And then his lips began to gently explore the contour of her neck, one hand softly stroking her back. And then he kissed her.

She met his lips eagerly, her heart pounding. Energy soared and coursed through her body as their lips welded together, and she thought her heart, or her head, or both would explode from the delicious ecstasy of his closeness and his intimacy. The woman in her responded with a pent-up passion that only twice before had been realised, but that had always been locked within her, with this man holding the key.

He moaned softly, and she felt a hand move to the zipper of her dress and draw it downward easily. His hand sought and found the soft swelling curve of her breast. She couldn't stop him. No— didn't want to. She had never known the exhilaration a touch could bring. The shivers ran up and down her spine, and her whole being tingled with a delight that she had not, even in her wildest imaginings, known existed.

Then without warning, he thrust her away from him, turning a ravaged face towards his window. She stared with wide-eyed hurt at his heaving shoulders. 'I'm sorry,' he said coldly, 'I shouldn't have done that.'

She concentrated quickly on the zipper, fighting the tears stinging behind her lashes. 'Dallas——'

'Cory,' he cut her off harshly, 'go into the house before something happens that I'd regret for the rest of my life.'

A bitter sob caught in her throat, but she controlled it with a supreme effort. She scrambled from the truck, stopping and looking back at him with what she hoped were icy eyes.

'I just thought I owed you something for the dinner,' she breathed bitterly, knowing the explanation was as much for herself as it was for him. 'Can you imagine that?' she hissed cruelly. 'I almost sold my soul to a two-bit cowboy!' She slammed the truck door violently and walked proudly to the house.

In her room, she let the tears flow freely. Why would he have regretted it for the rest of his life? she wondered in bitter confusion. Because he didn't love her, she admitted slowly. What other explanation could there be? That oblique reference to settling down had had nothing to do with her—though possibly it had something to do with whoever he was seeing when he left the ranch at nights. And the magic of the dinner and the dancing had existed only in her mind.

And she loved him, she thought with anguish. She loved him enough that she would have,

without hesitation or regret, given herself to him.
She wondered if he knew her better than she knew
herself, and if he had understood, instinctively,
what giving would have meant to her. It would
have had to have meant forever or it would have
destroyed her. And Dallas Hawthorne didn't
want forever. At least not with her.

She felt a fool for having let down her defences
one more time. Why, when she had known it
would end like this? With a hurt so raw and aching
she doubted that it would ever go away.

'Because I love him,' she whispered, and that
love defied reason and annihilated her self-control.
'What am I going to do?' she murmured brokenly.
'What on earth am I going to do?'

'Cory, are you going to sleep all day?'

Cory's eyes felt leaden, as if she hadn't slept at
all, when she opened them to see Tilda standing in
her doorway looking at her reprovingly.

'What time is it?' she groaned.

'Almost lunch time, for goodness sake.'

Lunch time. Dallas would be in soon. She didn't
think she could bear to sit through lunch with him.

'I don't want lunch,' she said heavily, and seeing
Tilda's concern, added hastily and more lightly, 'I
ate enough last night to last me for a week.'

Tilda's gaze was assessing. 'How was everything
last night?'

'Simply wonderful,' Cory replied dully.

'You were quite late. I thought you must be
having a good time, though I must say Dallas
didn't look very happy this morning. Maybe
because he had to get up and go to work, instead
of lazing around in bed all day.'

'Maybe,' Cory agreed through tight lips.
Naturally, Dallas would go to work. Just as if

nothing had happened. And at lunch he'd laugh and talk just as if nothing had happened. Just as if he hadn't taken her fragile heart and shattered it. Just as if he hadn't sucked her in one more time.

She dressed slowly, increasingly aware that she simply couldn't bear to see him. The humiliation and the hurt were tight in her throat, and if he so much as looked at her, she knew she would start to cry.

'Tilda, I'm going to grab an apple and go for a ride.' She forced her tone to be light.

Tilda turned and looked at her dubiously. 'Are you sure you're all right?' She surveyed Cory's wan face. 'Did you drink too much last night?' she asked shrewdly.

'We did drink quite a bit,' Cory said, not at all guilty about sending Tilda off on the wrong track. Far better that Tilda think both she and Dallas were suffering the ill effects of too much to drink, than to risk her start probing in an area Cory didn't feel she could ever talk about.

Tilda sighed. 'Would you pick up the mail for me on your way out?'

She rode down to the mailbox at the end of the lane, removed its contents and sifted through them without any real interest.

She stopped at one addressed to Shorty and frowned uneasily at the return address. What business could Shorty possibly have with the United States Army?

Absolutely none, a little voice warned her. This had something to do with Dallas, and the ridiculous feud Shorty insisted on playing out. She thought crazily she should put it in her pocket and steam it open before she handed it over. Or let it slide out of her hand and blow away as if it had never arrived.

She laughed a little shakily at what she was contemplating. Tampering with the mail was against the law. And much as she wanted to know what was in this official looking brown envelope, she didn't particularly cotton to the idea of going to jail for it.

Reluctantly, she slid the letter back into the heap. Should she tell Dallas? She squinted thoughtfully and then reminded herself bitterly that she wasn't on speaking terms with Dallas. He was quite capable of looking after himself anyway.

And there was always the chance she was once again letting her imagination get away from her. After all, she was certainly not up-to-date on Shorty's personal life and history. He could very well have legitimate business with the senders of this letter. Maybe they were contracting a large shipment of beef.

It was none of her business, she told herself firmly, dismissing it from her mind as she dropped off the letters at the house.

It was a beautiful sunshiny day, but Cory barely noticed, as she subconsciously turned Wings away from the pond, heading instead along the thickly wooded trail that would eventually bring her to the upper range lands and the outer reaches of the ranch.

Without wanting to, but unable to control herself, she relived the past evening in all its sweetness. Dallas' mellow voice as he'd talked about the ranch of his childhood, the way his eyes had lingered on her face, warm and appreciative, throughout the meal. She thought of the way it had felt to dance with him, the thrill of his hard body so close to hers, it's heat searing through the thin film of her dress.

She tortured herself, going over it again in her

mind. At one point it had even seemed like he loved her.

'No,' he'd said softly, 'I think my drifting days are about over.'

She had been so sure at that moment that all her conclusions about him had been right. That he'd been afraid of loving her, explaining his studied indifference to her, and his stinging cruelty. She'd also been sure that he had finally surrendered, this iron-willed man that she loved, to a feeling that not all of his determination or resolve had been able to crush.

She had felt it, she thought, in everything he had done. In the way he'd looked at her, in the way his soft drawl had been laced with tenderness, in the way his lips had pressed gently into her hair while they'd danced.

Even in the way that he had motioned for her to slide over beside him in the truck, as if it could be no other way. And his lips had been eager and possessive and gentle. His hand had found its way to her breast naturally, as though he acknowledged in spirit and in flesh she belonged to him, and he to her.

Cory brushed impatiently at the tears that were streaming down her cheeks. What a fool she was! An over-imaginative and naïve little fool.

Dallas' face came back to her, harsh and contemptuous. The rest of the night dissolved for her because of that moment. She shivered, certain that he had hated in that moment. Hated himself, for seducing a virgin, and her for being so without scruples to stop him.

Her face grew hot, partly from the remembered sensation, mostly from shame. All her ideas about decency and good and bad were oddly jumbled. How could anyone fight something that felt so incredibly wonderful? That was so deliciously and exquisitely overpowering things like reason and rules?

But he had fought it, she reminded herself, and her stomach turned queasily. How could she ever look at him again without longing for those strong, and oddly gently hands to claim her? How could she ever look at him again without feeling the hurt, shame and incredible sense of loss at his rejection?

She had to get away from him, she decided suddenly. That was it. She would ask Mac to send her to Europe ahead of him. Or maybe she could stay with that distant cousin who lived in Montreal for a while——

Cory suddenly became aware that Wings was prancing nervously, and throwing her head. She looked around feeling vaguely uneasy. They had broken into a large pasture some time ago and were in the middle of it now. She was aware suddenly of a closeness in the air—a strange static feeling.

The sun was gone she realised and she lifted her eyes to the sky and gasped at the boiling, angry black clouds that were rolling in billowing, ominous waves over the tree tops at the far edge of the field.

Hail clouds, she thought urgently, and dug her heels into Wings, the trees on the other side of the pasture suddenly seeming a long way off.

Thunder cracked and a ragged bolt of lightning ripped through the sky. The heavens opened and the hard stones of ice hissed down, hitting the ground with such force that they leaped back up two and three feet in the air. Cory felt the pain as they bounced off her, growing alarmingly large as the sudden storm's fury increased.

The next bolt of lightning almost blinded her it

was so close. It hit a tall, dead tree that stood alone in the middle of the pasture, splitting it with an ear-shattering crack. The dry, dead wood burst into flame.

A thought flashed wildly through her mind that she was lucky it hadn't been her, but even as she thought it she struggled to regain control of a furiously lunging Wings. Suddenly everything slowed down in her mind. Wings rearing, and snorting, pawing the air—her back legs sliding on the muddy ground, the earth rising, her own instinctive reaction of kicking out of the stirrups and leaping free of the falling horse.

Her head hurt, she thought with detachment, as she watched Wings frantically regain her feet, her eyes rolling with panic as the hailstones continued to pelt her frothing black coat. Cory followed her with her eyes as she charged across the field into the trees. Wings wasn't hurt, and neither rein had been dragging, Cory thought with relief.

She closed her eyes, pressing her face into the cool mud. She could feel the hailstones pummelling her, but oddly she could feel no pain. And then it seemed like the black mud oozed up over the top of her and swallowed her, for all went dark, and she felt no more.

CHAPTER EIGHT

WHEN she opened her eyes the ground around her was deep in shadow. The sky, once again blue and innocent looking, was beginning to darken with the swiftly approaching night.

Cory moved tentatively, and groaned, her head swimming and her entire body aching from the beating it had sustained from the hailstones. A jolt of fear passed through her. She felt entirely too weak to move, but bear sightings were not uncommon in this region, and even the usually timid coyotes might circle her as easy prey. She looked around warily to see if any yellow eyes were gleaming at her from now sinister looking underbrush.

Her ears strained against the silence, magnifying the woodland sounds all around her to terrifying proportions. Suddenly her whole body tensed with alertness. She was sure she had heard the faint sounds of a large animal, probably on the same trail through the woods that she had used earlier.

She fixed frightened eyes on those far off trees, waiting, her heart hammering in her throat. But it was not a bear that broke from the trees. She went weak with relief. Even though the horse and rider were completely black-shadowed and without detail, she recognised them instantly. He stopped and she could see tension in his outline, in the way he cocked his head alertly.

'Cory!'

His voice held the urgent treble note of fear,

Cory thought abstractedly, but of course that wasn't possible. Dallas was the one who handled emergencies with such unflappable calm.

'Dallas,' she called hoarsely, afraid her voice wouldn't carry, it sounded so thin and feeble in her own ears. But his head swivelled towards her, and with roughness and impatience she'd never seen him use on Raiser he jerked the horse around and spurred him incautiously over the dark, uneven pasture.

She struggled to a sitting position, ignoring the explosions of light the effort set off in the back of her head. Dallas yanked the horse to a skidding halt in front of her, and was out of the saddle and balanced on his heels in front of her in a single liquid motion.

His face was forbidding, she thought, shrinking from him. His mouth was a strained, firm white line, and his eyes were furious. Though his hands rested on his knees, they were clenching and unclenching tightly and she had the oddest sensation he wanted to shake her.

'Are you all right?' he finally asked, the voice constrained and low.

She nodded uncertainly, and he scanned her face, lifted a strong finger to her chin, and firmly guided her head one way and then the other. His finger touched near her temple and she winced, aware of his eyes suddenly sharply on her own. He ran a finger over her muddy cheek, stopping abruptly when she winced again.

'You little fool!' he hissed, his voice shaking with barely controlled fury.

He was angry about last night, she thought cloudily, her eyes wide on his face. He was angry that he'd had to come and find her. It was so unfair. It wasn't her fault that she'd fallen off her horse, or that there'd been a storm. He shouldn't be angry.

'Don't be mad at me, Dallas,' she pleaded weakly, narrowing her eyes because his face seemed to be fading from in front of her.

Did he look suddenly stricken? Or were her eyes playing tricks on her? Her other senses were playing tricks on her, too, because as he lifted her and held her cradled in his arms, she could have sworn he was trembling. Maybe it was her own trembling she felt—she was aware suddenly of being terribly cold. But even her ears seemed to be having some fun with her.

'I'm not mad at you, darling. I was just scared. I was just so damned scared.' His voice seemed faded, and faraway and dream-like. What a funny thing the mind was, she thought wearily, making up something like that. Dallas, she thought fuzzily, didn't get scared. Then as if to confirm it, hers went black again.

She opened her eyes and stared, bewildered, at the unfamiliar ceiling. She turned her head cautiously and looked around the sun-bathed, tiny room, recognising it finally as one of the line shacks.

Her head hurt, and she reached up, and found it bound with a bandage. The rest of her hurt, too, and the rough wool blanket scratched. With sudden, stupefying awareness she realised that it was her naked flesh against that blanket.

She remembered hazily and uneasily Dallas finding her last night. For a minute she felt warm and happy. Had he called her darling? The happiness faded swiftly. Surely he hadn't undressed her?

The door swung open, and Dallas walked in, glanced at her, and dropped an armload full of wood by the door. He came over and studied her sternly, and she shrank from his gaze, pulling the coarse blanket up around her neck.

'How are you feeling?' he asked coolly.

Her cheeks flamed. 'Where are my clothes?' she croaked.

He jerked his head towards the stove, and she saw her underwear draped boldly over the back of a chair.

'You were soaked to the skin. I didn't have any choice. How are you feeling?'

'I want to die,' she muttered, mortally embarrassed.

'You haven't got anything I haven't seen before,' he said clinically, and without sympathy. 'And you're not going to die. As far as I can see you're bruised from head to toe——' he looked annoyed at her deepening blush '—and you've got concussion.'

This man certainly hadn't called her darling last night, she thought grimly. He seemed completely indifferent to her.

'Why did we come here? Why didn't we go home?'

His eyes narrowed at her implication. 'We came here,' he responded tersely, 'because it was close. It was moonless last night, my horse was exhausted—and you were chilled to the bone. I'm sorry if your virtue had to be considered secondary.'

Was that a snide reference to the other night? she wondered unhappily. Her virtue had seemed rather secondary at that moment, too. Dallas seemed distinctly unhappy about their being thrown together like this. Only yesterday she'd been plotting how to never see him again. From the look on his face now, she wished it would have worked out.

'When are we leaving?' she asked, striving to match his coldness.

'We'll have something to eat first. Then I'll decide if you're up to the trip.' He ignored the defiant flash in her eyes. 'When was the last time you ate?'

'I had an apple yesterday,' she offered weakly.

'God Almighty, Cory!' He turned impatiently from her, took her clothes from where they hung on an assortment of chair backs, and flung them down on the bed beside her.

'I'm not getting dressed with you in here,' she protested stubbornly. She thought she detected the faintest flicker of amusement in his eyes, and flushed.

'I'll keep my back turned,' he said with carefully controlled patience. Abruptly he swung away from her, picked up the armload of wood by the door, and began stoking the stove.

Even so, Cory dressed awkwardly under the covers, her eyes glued to his broad back. Her clothes, she noticed with surprise, were not just dry but clean, and she was a little taken aback at this apparently tender gesture.

He turned and watched her assessingly as she made her way, a trifle shakily, across to the bare wooden table, and sank down.

The line shacks always contained supplies, and she studied him from under the veil of her lashes as he mixed together pancake ingredients. For the first time she noticed his face was grey-lined with fatigue, and that there was strain in the firm set of his lips, and tautness in his features.

She ate more because she was afraid not to, than because of any real appetite. Dallas' expression was stony and uninviting, and they ate in what Cory found to be uncomfortable silence.

'I'll do the dishes,' she volunteered timidly, when they were done.

'You'll stay put,' he snapped, with unnecessary irritation.

'Are you always such a bear in the morning?' she flashed back.

'What the hell do you expect!' His voice cracked like thunder through the tiny cabin, and Cory stared at him stunned. She had seen him angry before, but never like this. She had never heard him raise his voice, and her heart quailed at the fury that had darkened his eyes to stormy blue-black.

He stood up and her eyes trailed up his mountainous frame. His legs, set wide apart, were braced with tension, and she could see the muscle clearly outlined through the moulded fabric of his jeans. His stomach was narrow and flat and taut, expanding into the deep broadness of his chest, and the tense expanse of his shoulders. She felt it now, too. A physical tension like electricity in the air between them. It wasn't, she realised, just fury in those eyes.

Her eyes returned to his face, and her breath caught in her throat. Swiftly he crossed to her side, glaring down at her. And then with a savage moan, he wrapped his hand in her hair forcing her head back, and dropped his lips with punishing force over hers. All his tension, and worry, and fear were inherent in that feral kiss.

He broke away from her, some of his tension eased, replaced by weariness. 'I'm sorry,' he said thickly.

'You don't have to be,' she responded softly.

'Damn it, Cory! I'm a man. Don't tempt me beyond my limit!'

She would have liked very much to brazenly

tempt him beyond his limit. But his eyes held
warning, and she was suddenly awkwardly aware
of her gaucheness, her total lack of experience, her
total innocence, and the dull pain in her head.

'Why don't you wait for me on the porch?' he
suggested, almost gently. 'I won't be long.'

Without looking at him, she nodded her
agreement and went out into the morning
sunshine. She didn't, she acknowledged forlornly,
know very much about men. That Dallas desired
her was obvious. But given the rather intimate
circumstances of last night, would he have felt the
same way with any woman?

Desire wasn't love, she told herself. And yet she
knew she couldn't possibly feel one without the
other. Was it the same for a man? She somehow
doubted it.

Men were supposed to have less control than
women, she rembered from some girlish high
school chit-chat, and yet it was Dallas who always
showed more control. Why? Because he thought of
her as a child? Or respected her? Or didn't like her
enough? Or simply because he knew how deeply
committed she would become to him after, and
wasn't prepared for that?

He came out of the cabin, and stepped over her
without even a glance. She sighed, watching him
with wistful and longing eyes as he saddled Raiser.
He mounted, and she rose. He rode over, leaned
down and grasped her securely under her arms,
swinging her lithely into the cradle of his arms.

'I'd rather ride behind,' she muttered
mutinously, leaning her head into the hollow of his
shoulder, and glaring at him as if to deny how her
heart pounded at being so close to him.

'You'll do as I damn well see fit,' he returned
tightly, not even glancing at her. She might have

argued, save for the sudden wave of dizziness that made her admit reluctantly to the wisdom of her present position.

'Have you seen Wings?' she asked as they headed out. 'Did she go back to the ranch?'

'Yes,' he said without elaboration, but she saw a muscle in his jaw twitch, and guessed that the memory of the riderless horse coming into the yard had not been a good one. Not that that meant he felt anything for her—a riderless horse was pretty grim business no matter who was involved.

'How'd it happen?' he asked, and she felt the hard muscle of his stomach tighten, though his voice had been calm to the point of being uninterested.

She told him, and felt the tension release in his belly. 'What did you think happened?' she asked softly.

'Tilda gave me a rather brutal tongue-lashing about feeding you too much booze the night before. She figured your reactions were probably out enough that you got thrown.'

Cory coloured uncomfortably. 'But you knew I wasn't hungover.'

'Hangovers aren't the only thing that can affect concentration and reaction time. You should have seen that storm coming, Cory.'

'Hail storms hit pretty fast,' she retorted defensively.

'Not that fast,' he snapped tersely.

Suddenly she remembered his coldly controlled fury when he'd found her. 'You think it was my own fault!' she breathed with horrified indignation.

'I didn't say that,' he responded coolly.

'You thought it, though,' she accused angrily.

'As a matter of fact, that's not what I thought, so I'll thank you not to try and read my mind.'

She scowled at him, but then something in the haggard lines of his face sparked slow understanding. 'Did you think it was your fault?' She struggled against a wave of dizziness, but nothing escaped his alert eyes.

'Quit talking so much,' he ordered gruffly. 'We'll talk about it when you're feeling better.' He hesitated, his eyes suddenly softer on her face. 'I think we've got quite a lot to talk about when you're feeling better.'

'Do we?' she asked tiredly, but it took quite a lot of effort to get those words out. Feeling safe, and secure and contented she fell asleep.

She awoke once, with some urgent dream flitting evasively around her somehow fogged brain. She looked up into Dallas' face. It had something to do with him. She had to tell him something. About a letter, she thought fuzzily, suddenly uncertain if it was real or part of a dream.

'Are you okay?' he asked, instantly aware she had awakened, his eyes alert and observant on her face despite the tiny etched lines of weariness around them.

'Your eyes are very blue,' she whispered, not really sure if she was still dreaming or awake. Her mind felt funny—like a cloud drifting.

He said nothing.

'You know what the morning sky looks like, Dallas? Just before the sun comes up? When the black melts into that intense shade of blue?'

'Ssssh, Cory,' he said gently.

'But I have to tell you something.' She felt that, again, quite urgently. But she couldn't remember exactly what. A letter? Or that she loved him?

'It'll wait, Cory,' he said with gentle firmness.

She felt quite relieved, because she suddenly felt very, very tired.

She felt confused when she awoke again. The rocking motion that had lulled and comforted her had stopped, and there were so many voices. She opened her eyes cautiously and was overwhelmed.

Tilda. Mac. Cameron. Shelly. The Jacobsens. The Stubbs. There were horses, weary-looking and dusty all through the yard.

'What are all these people doing here?' she asked aware of them coming towards her and Dallas. Tilda was crying—so were Shelly and Mrs Stubbs.

'I think they were all looking for you.'

'All night?' she gasped.

'Some are probably still out.'

'That makes me feel awful,' she said shakily.

'Don't Cory. You're well-loved. That should only feel good.'

Gently he passed her down to Cameron. 'Get her to bed. And get a doctor.' He swung out of the saddle, and she watched a knot of people forming around him, all talking at once, all asking questions.

He's so tired, she thought. Can't you people see how tired he is? Just leave him alone.

Nancy burst out of the house, racing by her and Cameron and Tilda, her eyes seeing only the man across the yard. Her legs were so long and slim in her tight jeans, Cory noted. She looked so beautiful with her black hair flying behind her as she ran.

She twisted in Cameron's arms, looking bleakly over his shoulder. Nancy threw her arms around Dallas' neck, and kissed him long and hard on the mouth.

Cory shuddered and close her eyes. Her head

hurt. All these people had been worried about her. Tilda was crying. Dallas and Nancy. She began to cry.

Cory slammed down the cards she was playing with, restlessly. She knew she was really well enough to be up and about, but her bedroom seemed to be as good a hiding place as any.

She didn't remember very much about Dallas finding her, or about their ride down to the ranch, but she had a terribly uneasy feeling that she'd said something to him that she shouldn't have. Like that she loved him.

The very possibility made her flush, especially since she could distinctly remember him saying they had to talk about some things, and since she could very distinctly remember the way he had greeted Nancy. That didn't leave her with very much doubt about what Dallas wanted to say to her.

He had been up to see her every-day, no doubt out of some ridiculous sense of duty, and his attitude had confirmed her suspicions. A kind of gentle, concerned attitude, which was exactly what she would expect from a man who had the terrible task of explaining realities to the foolish girl who had lost her heart to him. No doubt, he would lose no time in letting her down easily once the opportunity presented itself.

So far he hadn't had the chance. There'd alwayst been somebody else in the room, or else she'd pretended to be quite a bit groggier than she was. Sooner or later, she realised with a sigh, she was going to have to face up to it, but right now she didn't feel strong enough.

Cory picked up the picture off the table beside her bed and studied it for about the thousandth time, and smiled softly at the wrinkled red face that looked back at her. Travis Jess Scott. 'I'll be home Wednesday,' Shelly's handwriting read. 'Call me.'

With a start, Cory realised it was Wednesday, and eagerly picked up the phone beside her bed. She hadn't heard the phone ring, so she was surprised it was being used. She went to hang up when the urgency in the soft, drawling feminine voice stopped her.

'When did you become so cruel, Dallas?' The line was staticky and the voice far away.

His laugh was bitter and completely without humour. 'Do you want a date?'

'Dallas, you must come.' Cory realised the voice belonged to someone around Tilda's age.

'I can't.'

'Don't you mean you won't?' The voice sounded weary, heart-broken, and resigned.

'Have it your way then. I won't.'

Cory replaced the receiver like it was hot, realising with a sudden flash of horrible guilt that she had no business eavesdropping on such a personal conversation. Still, the bit she had heard upset her enough that she forgot all about calling Shelly.

How could she love a man capable of such coldness and cruelty, she asked herself? And yet she knew why. Because the cruelty had been created. It was at odds with the side of Dallas that she'd seen much more of—the confident, charismatic, gentle and warm Dallas. The only real problem was what had created it, if he'd ever trust her enough to tell her, so that she could help make it go away.

A purely theoretical speculation, she reminded herself wearily, because all Dallas wanted to tell her was that he didn't love her.

*   *   *

'Hi, there.'

Cory looked up from her book, startled. Tilda had told her earlier that everyone was going to the movies, and she had assumed that included Dallas. She had rather eagerly shed her housecoat, got dressed, and taken advantage of her freedom to get out of her room and come downstairs.

'Let's go for a walk,' Dallas suggested when she didn't reply. 'It's beautiful out. It's snowing.'

Her eyes flew to the window, and sure enough the large, wet snowflakes were bright against the sky.

'I don't think so, Dallas,' she replied in her best invalid voice. 'I'm still not feeling very well.'

'You should have been up long ago, and you know it,' he said quietly, his eyes amused.

'Pardon me!' she retorted heatedly. 'I didn't realise you were a doctor.'

'Actually, I'm just repeating what the doctor told Tilda at dinner tonight,' he said evenly.

'Well, I'm still not going for a walk. It's snowing, it's the middle of the night,' she flushed under his raised eyebrow—it was only eight o'clock, 'and I wouldn't go anywhere with you!'

'We're going for a walk,' he said with unnerving firmness.

'Drop dead, Dallas!' She glared as he impatiently threw open the coat cupboard door, tugged a sweater down from a hook, and turned back to her. 'I'm not——' she began heatedly.

He was in front of her in a single long stride. Wordlessly, he stooped, picked her up with one strong arm, and threw her carelessly over his shoulder. He straightened, oblivious to her indignant squeal, and to her pounding on the small of his back. But even as she struggled something inside her had long ago surrendered,

and betrayed her now, by causing her heart to beat
wildly at the touch of his broad shoulders, and his
burning arm around her legs.

Finally, outside and half way across the yard, he
flipped her back off his shoulder and set her down,
handing her sweater to her.

She snatched it from him, and put it on,
regarding him with flashing eyes.

'What do you want?' she hissed, not giving in in
the slightest to the magic of the wonderful light
snowflakes dancing around them.

'I already told you. I want to go for a walk,' he
stated simply, looking down at her with dark,
mirth-filled eyes.

'Definitely not!' Cory spat at him. 'Now I know
that you're crazy, as well as being insufferably
arrogant and conceited!' Not bothered in the least,
he took her unwilling hand and towed her along
behind him.

He took a deep breath. 'This is one of my
favourite things about this area,' he said softly.
'It's as wild and unpredictable as a two-year-old
filly. Snow in the summer. Imagine that.'

'I don't have to imagine it,' Cory snapped,
trying to pull her hand from his firm grasp. 'I'm
walking through it, and I'd prefer not to be.'

Suddenly Dallas stopped, cupping her face in his
large hands and smiling as the moonbeams and
snowflakes played across it, revealing her confusion. Slowly, he bent and kissed her.

Furiously, she fought him, struggling with
everything she had not to give in to the temptation
of his lips. Finally, she managed to break from his
grasp, and she pulled away and stood panting and
eyeing him wildly.

'Tell me you don't love me,' he commanded
softly. 'Tell me that, if you can.'

'I don't——' she sputtered, and then faltered, looking desperately away from him. The fight oozed out of her. Did he have to do it like this? Couldn't he find a better way to let her down? One that would leave her with a shred of dignity? 'Why, Dallas?' she whispered, in a tortured voice. 'Why must you torment me?'

He was in front of her, and his arms went smoothly around her. 'Tell me you love me,' he ordered softly, his awesome eyes resting on her upturned face.

'No,' she protested breathlessly, and started to cry helplessly. 'Why is that so important to you?' she sobbed. 'Why must you insist I tell you I love you? Please just tell me what you have to say and get it over with.'

'All right, Cory,' he agreed tenderly. 'I love you.'

Her eyes widened, and met his still sparkling with tears. 'Please don't say that, Dallas.'

'I have to. I love you.'

'But Nancy,' she stammered uncertainly. 'The way she kissed you . . .'

'She was most disappointed that her kiss wasn't returned in kind.'

'Wasn't it?' Cory whispered.

'Of course it wasn't. I love you.'

He'd said it again, she thought stupidly. 'But—but, you were so mean to me when you found me. And in the cabin——'

'Cory! I was crazy with worry when I found you. And furious at myself—not you. And that morning in the cabin all I wanted to do was hold you, and love you, and make you mine.' He grinned, teasingly. 'Fortunately, or unfortunately, someone passing out while I'm making love to them doesn't really appeal to me.'

'But the night before you could have——'

His expression was pained, and a low growl came from his throat. 'Cory I wanted you, and loved you, and you were so damned eager and willing.

'But I didn't want you like that. Not after you'd had too much wine, and certainly not in the front seat of a pick-up truck. Can you understand, Cory?' His tone was soft and caressing.

He continued softly when she didn't answer. 'I want the first time to be so special for you. I want you on a big feather bed, with silk sheets, and the moon streaming across your body. I want to wake up the next morning with you cuddled up beside me, and my arms wrapped around you.

'And I don't want there to be any guilt or shame. I want you to know that nothing in this world was ever as right or as good as us loving each other.

'I want you to marry me, Cory.'

She studied his face cautiously, trying to understand, trying to believe. And then the light shining deep in his eyes told her what she had been afraid to believe from his lips. It was true, she thought dazedly, it was true! Something inside her slowly began to come awake, and the ice fell from her heart and was replaced by fire.

Her eyes began to shine with incredible lustre, and an unbidden smile lit her lips. He pulled her close against him, and she rejoiced in the warmth she felt there in the shadow of his heart.

'I love you,' she murmured contentedly against his chest. 'Oh, God Dallas, I love you so much.'

He stroked her hair gently, holding her close against his hard frame. Then swiftly, he let her go, throwing a handful of snow in her face, and running laughing from her. Like two young deer, they dashed through the snow, their laughter pealing crisply through the snowy summer night.

She wadded snowballs, laughing with delight when the odd one hit him, and not caring that most of them missed. His aim was deadly accurate, and finally fed up with losing, she crept up behind him and stuffed huge handfuls of snow down his shirt on to the warm skin of his back.

Laughing she dashed away from him, collapsing merrily against the cushion of snow when his strong arms wrapped around her legs, dropping her.

Suddenly, it was so quiet. He was looking down at her with wonder, her head cushioned in the white snow, her eyes wide and dark and joyous against it. He kissed her neck gently, and then his lips explored her face with tender small kisses. He pulled her out of the snow and brushed it from her clothes, then he drew her into his arms once more. She raised her lips expectantly to his, and his kiss was long and sweet, passionate and possessive.

'Dallas,' she said later, still leaning into him hungrily and relishing in the feel of his strong body touching hers, 'I thought all week that you were going to tell me that you loved Nancy. It did seem like you felt something for her, and I was so afraid to hear what it was.'

'You know what it was, Cory? I was hurt once from loving people. Hurt so badly I swore nobody would ever come that close to me again. The warning bells went off inside me the first time I saw you spitting at me like a ferocious kitten. And I ignored them.

'But after I kissed you that night on the porch I could no longer deny how vulnerable I was to you, so I put up my defences. I ignored you and sought out a girl like Nancy. A hard girl, who couldn't hurt me, and who I couldn't hurt.

'That should have been the end of it. Except that I already cared enough about you that I felt like it was my duty to discourage you from throwing away your life on Timmy Stubbs. Or that's what I told myself. More honestly, my motives were selfishly male. If I couldn't have you, nobody else was going to, either.

'I fought my feelings every inch of the way, Cory, and failed. Being in the same room with you was torture, being away from you was worse. I knew how you were feeling, and I knew I was hurting you. I told myself that I didn't care. But my insides felt like they were going through a paper shredder.

'Then the day I asked you out for dinner, after one more sleepless night, I finally came to my senses. I realised that after all these years it was time to take a chance again.' He paused, looking at her intently.

'Cory, I'm a worse cripple than Missy will ever be. I want to think you can make it different, but I don't know if it's curable after all these years. You'd be taking a chance, too, and I want you to know the whole story before you make up your mind about whether or not you're going to spend the rest of your life with me.'

'What happened to you?' she asked wide-eyed, taking in the pain that contorted his handsome features with horror. 'Dallas, what happened?'

He shook his head. 'It's late, Cory.' He touched the dark little smudges under her eyes tenderly. 'We'll talk tomorrow.' He hesitated and added softly, 'And if you change your mind, I'll understand.'

'Dallas,' she said firmly, 'I've already made up my mind, and nothing could ever make me change it. Nothing!'

'We'll see,' he said almost impatiently, and the sudden ice in his voice ran like a shiver up and down her spine.

CHAPTER NINE

TILDA, Mac, Shorty and Dutch were back from the movies and engaged in a game of cribbage when Dallas and Cory came in, shaking the snow from their hair and clothes.

'Cory!' Tilda reproved. 'I couldn't figure out where on earth you had got to. When I left you were in bed, hardly able to move, and——' She stopped suddenly, her eyes moving to Cory and Dallas' intertwined hands. Her eyes were sparkling knowingly as they returned to Cory's face, and surveyed approvingly her high-coloured cheeks, and glowing, luminous eyes.

'Oh,' she breathed softly, 'so that's the way it is.'

'Tilda, it's your go,' Mac said impatiently. He turned and looked at Cory and Dallas. 'The way what is?'

Cory hesitated. Dallas had said he wanted to talk to her about some things, but she knew that she wasn't going to change her mind, and besides Tilda seemed to have already guessed. She couldn't keep this wonderful, bubbling feeling all to herself anyway.

'Dallas asked me to marry him.'

Tilda squealed, her cards going high in the air. She was out of her chair and had enveloped Cory in a bear hug with a speed that seemed impossible in a woman her size.

She released Cory and waltzed over to Dallas. He too, was subjected to her crushing hug, and he acknowledged her husky congratulations with a soft thank you.

'Mac.' He released Tilda. 'Mac, with your blessing, I'd like to marry your daughter.'

Mac's mouth opened, and closed and opened again. 'My daughter?' he finally squeaked incredulously.

Cory moved to Dallas, and he took her hand and held it tightly as they both waited for Mac's reply.

'Well, I'll be goll-durned,' Mac muttered with a shake of his head. He stared at his cards. Suddenly he turned and glared sternly at Dallas. 'Do you know what I'm holding?'

'No, sir,' Dallas replied, puzzled.

'Twenty-nine,' Mac informed him woefully. 'A perfect hand. You know what I would have said if somebody told me yesterday I'd hold a twenty-nine and not play it?'

'No, sir,' Dallas replied, beginning to smile.

'Would have told them there weren't no news in this old world good enough to keep me from playing at twenty-nine.' He grinned. 'Would have been wrong, too.' With an ear-splitting whoop, he threw the cards roofwards.

Cory rushed into his arms, and he picked her up and whirled her around.

'I told you,' he rasped a little breathlessly when he finally set her down, 'I told you this would happen the day you brung home that foamy dress. Good thing,' he added gruffly, 'I been preparing myself. Hell, I don't even feel misty.'

Cory placed a quick hand over the smile that tugged at her lips. For a man who didn't feel 'misty' Mac's eyes were strangely wet around the edges.

He turned from her quickly and extended a hand to Dallas. 'Congratulations—son,' he exclaimed softly.

'Thanks, Mac.' His and Mac's eyes locked, and Cory felt wonderfully contented at the look of mutual affection and respect that passed between them.

Dutch came over to Cory. 'I ain't misty either,' he proclaimed defensively, taking a swipe at his brimming eyes with his sleeve. He took her shoulders and looked deep into her eyes. Then he planted a firm kiss on her cheek. 'Be happy,' he said simply.

He turned to Dallas, and eyed him appraisingly, and then with a grin, extended his hand and pumped Dallas' energetically. 'I wouldn't say this to many men you understand, but Cory's pretty special to me. She deserves the best. And I think she got it.'

'That a fact?' Shorty scoffed, and Cory whirled to face him. An ugly sneer had twisted his face, and she gasped at the wickedness she saw there. With sudden clarity she remembered that letter, and felt suddenly and sinkingly that she should have told Dallas about it after all.

'It's a fact,' Dutch said, folding his arms firmly across his chest, and giving Shorty a puzzled, wary look.

Shorty pulled a file nonchalantly from his back pocket and carefully began cleaning his nails. He was aware of, and obviously relishing in, the expectant silence. Finally he slid Dallas a wily look, and then looked back at his nails.

'Quite a catch, aren't you, Tex?' he gloated, and there was no mistaking now the mocking in his tone, or the smugness in his face.

'If you've got something to say, get on with it,' Dallas snapped tersely.

'Think there'd be all this fuss if they knew the truth about you, Tex?'

'What truth might you be talking about?' Dallas asked calmly, but Cory heard something there that made her turn to him wide-eyed. For all the deadly calm in his voice, the blood had drained from his face, and his eyes were brimming with fiery fury.

Shorty rose, and stretched, deliberately moving to put the table between himself and Dallas. A man less determined might have backed down from the lethal fury burning in those eyes that suddenly held more black than blue. Shorty hesitated, but then with more dogged determination than courage, he held Dallas' gaze.

'Cold as nails, aren't you? And harder than a rock. Course, I hear a man can get like that—on the inside.'

The inside? Cory thought frantically. The inside of what? That expression was used in a context. Of what? The army? No. Then she felt herself growing cold. She remembered. From some stupid movie or television show. Prison. The 'inside' meant prison.

'Yup,' Shorty said, reading her sudden paleness with cruel accuracy. 'The great Dallas Hawthorne, defender of women and children, and contender for the foreman's job, is an ex-con.'

It wasn't just that incident with Shelly, she thought dully. Shorty had been threatened by Dallas, thought he wanted his job. Even so, this was crazy and cruel, and not true. It couldn't be true.

She closed her eyes, fighting the terrible trembling of her heart. One look at Dallas will tell you, she told herself, one look will tell you if it's true or not. Slowly, she forced her eyes open, and looked at his strong, familiar profile. She breathed a sigh of relief.

'Tell him it's not true, Dallas,' she implored with

a shaky laugh, her eyes fixed pleadingly on his face. 'Tell poor Shorty what a fool he's been for making such a dreadful mistake.'

The silence grew frighteningly long.

'Dallas!' she cried, aware of the hysterical edge to her voice, but unable to contain it.

With an effort, he pulled his gaze from Shorty's face, shifting his focus slowly to her. She took a step back from the cold, killing fury in those eyes. But the expression faded quickly, replaced by weariness. His gaze moved past her, and he stared emotionlessly out the kitchen window.

'It's true,' he stated tightly.

She stood and stared at him, stunned. A voice from the past mocked her. 'I haven't robbed a corner store.' So what had it been? A bank? Horrified, she turned from him and ran for the door. She didn't stop running until she was out of range of the voices that had suddenly burst into life on her departure.

She caught a tree to keep her legs from buckling under her, hugging it until the coarseness bit into her cheek. The tears stung painfully behind her eyes, and then began to trickle slowly and sorrowfully down her mute face. Like a summer storm, the gentle downpour escalated until the tears raced down her face in a constant ribbon. Desperate, choking sobbing racked her body.

'Cory.'

She turned to the voice, her eyes wild and frightened like those of a startled deer. He emerged from the darkness, catching her shoulders, his eyes sweeping her face. He let go.

'I'm sorry,' he said softly.

'Go away, Dallas.' She turned from him harshly.

'I never meant for you to find out like this,

Cory. It's part of what I wanted you to know before you made up your mind.'

He had asked her to wait until she knew the whole story, she acknowledged, and yet still——

'I want you to listen to me now, Cory.'

'Isn't that kind of like closing the barn door after the horse is out?' she snapped, childish in her confusion, and sense of betrayal.

He sighed. 'Ex-con is a powerful word isn't it, Cory? It conjures up images—brutal images, of brutal men who murder and rape and rob. It wasn't like that. I'm not like that. I don't think you could have fallen in love with me if I was.'

She whirled and regarded him with flashing eyes. 'I suppose you're going to tell me you were innocent.'

'No,' he said slowly. 'Not innocent. Young.'

He lifted his head to the winking stars, and took a deep breath. 'So young,' he continued softly, 'that now it seems like that foolish proud kid was somebody else. It's a long story, Cory. And a hard one to tell. Will you hear me out?'

Her anger melted under his questioning gaze, and she nodded slowly.

He returned his gaze to the stars, hesitated and then began.

'I told you once that my father was an oilman. He was proud and prosperous and pompous—an empire builder and a king maker. He wanted, like most fathers, for me to be all that he was. But by the time he got around to noticing that I was alive and old enough to start grooming as his successor, I already knew I was a cowboy.

'I was about fifteen when he started to make his first overtures. He wanted me to take some business education courses. He wanted me to come into his office once a week—wearing a suit and tie no less—and he wanted me to spend some time around the oil rigs. Even then I had a stubborn streak in me that matched his, and in a few choice phrases I told him what I thought of the idea. And in a few choice phrases he taught me the meaning of power. I started to learn the business, or I was grounded. No horses, no communication with the ranch hands, nothing except the four walls of my room closing in around me. He won round one.

'Then the football stuff started. I was Garth Hawthorne's son, and that alone meant I should play football. I was also big and fast. I didn't care much for football, but I played. And I played my heart out, because I knew if I didn't he wouldn't hesitate to yank my horse out from under me until I shaped up.

'I guess I played too well. I was offered a try-out for the Texas University team. My dad was delighted. Football heroes make for good PR. Plus, I could get the business background I needed to make a real contribution to his business when I graduated. He still thought I was going to magically outgrow this thing about being a cowboy. He was wrong. I was eighteen, and I left.

'I went to find myself, which is what every kid in the country was doing at the time. But instead of wearing a guru shirt, and long hair, and beads, I was wearing a cowboy hat and boots, and carrying a battered up old saddle from one end of the country to the other, following the rodeos. I usually won enough money to eat once or twice a day, and call my mom once a week to tell a few lies about how well I was doing.

'I guess I knew there was a war on, but I was pretty wrapped up in how I was going to get to the next rodeo, and what bull I might draw to ride when I got there. Then the draft notice caught up with me.'

His tone changed, and Cory saw a muscle working in his jaw. She was rooted to her spot, listening to his words with uncontrollable compassion. She knew at last that he was unravelling his mystery for her, and she knew from his face and tone that it was painful and took a lot of trust. She felt she loved him more at this moment than she ever had before.

'Dad put all our differences behind him. Without even asking me, he had some senator friend looking into getting me into West Point. Maybe if he would have asked . . .

'But he didn't. He ordered, and I rebelled, and ended up taking orders all day everyday as a buck private in the infantry. And then our company got its orders. Vietnam.'

He stopped for a long time, staring into the darkness as if he could see ghosts darting among the shadows of the trees. The silence grew longer. His eyes suddenly flicked to her. 'I've never talked about it before. I think it's going to be harder than I thought.'

She nodded, her heart going out to him. His gaze, thoughtful and remote, moved back to the trees.

'We were just kids. Most of us hadn't been having for very long. Some of us weren't old enough to buy a beer in most states. Kids, too close to childhood, who'd always known safety and security, soft pillows, warm beds, milkshakes and steak sandwiches. Kids who'd always been able to run home to Mom's comforting arms when things got too scary.

And then suddenly, you're scared all the time and you can't run home. You're in this steaming hot jungle, and all you can think of is air-conditioned drugstores, and a coke with ice in it.

Because it's easier to think of that than to think somebody out there is going to kill you if he has the chance.

'Eventually, the fear fades. So do the images of cokes and air-conditioned drugstores. They're a part of another world, and nothing you learned in that other world is going to help you survive here.

'I was promoted to a platoon leader, more because I showed an uncanny knack for surviving than because I was a good soldier. I was determined that my men and I were going home alive and in one piece.

'We almost made it, too. Except that the next hand I got dealt was a bad one. We got a new officer. Melvin Rasmusen. I'd gone to school with him, but I didn't even know him. I should have had the good sense to pretend I recognised him, but I didn't.

'He took an understandable delight in having the old high school star having to address him as sir. I didn't blame him for that. I didn't even blame him for assigning me to every lousy job he could find.

'But then he masterminded this screwball idea for taking some little flag on his map. His approach was foolhardy and dangerous, and I told him so. I told him we'd lose more people than his little flag was worth. I'd never begged in my life, but I begged then. I didn't think I was asking for much, a little more thought, a few tactical changes. I didn't win one concession. The more I argued the more determined he became.

'We took that little flag, and we payed for it. I lost two of my best friends. One went home in a bag, the other minus a set of very good legs.'

He'd stopped again, and Cory remembered his fury that night that Shorty had asked about

Vietnam. She was beginning to understand some of the terrible things he wrestled with.

'We won through,' he continued wearily. 'And when we got back, there was all this back-slapping about what a fine job we'd done.

'Something snapped inside me. Rasmusen didn't have a chance. I attacked him. It took four men twelve minutes to pull me off him. In twelve minutes I broke his nose and three ribs. It was a bad mistake, but it wasn't the worst one.

'Melvin was pretty eager to have the whole incident hushed up, because he didn't want his leadership abilities to be investigated. He made me a decent offer. All I had to do was apologise to him, in front of my men, and it would go down in the books that he'd fallen down a concealed tunnel.

'I couldn't. Part of it was pride, and part of it was not knowing what the United States Army could do to me. I figured I'd get rapped on the knuckles, stripped of my stripes, and sent back to my company.

'Like I said, young. And stupid. Assaulting an officer in a combat zone is not taken lightly. I was shipped stateside, court-martialled and sentenced to a military prison.

'Within a week I knew I'd made the biggest mistake of my life by not apologising to Melvin. I would have got down on one knee before him to reverse what had happened. Two weeks in that hell-hole and, given the choice, I would have kissed his boots to get out of there. But choices were a thing of the past. I wasn't allowed choices. I didn't even have a name anymore—I had a number. It seemed like a hell of a price to pay for not keeping my temper in check.

'And it got higher. I got a letter from Dad. I didn't have to read it to know that it was bad news. I was put in a padded cell before they'd hand it over.

'I stared at it for a long time before I could find the guts to open it and read it. I guess I kind of knew what it was going to say. It was pretty straightforward. Not even a lecture about what a disappointment I was, or how I'd disgraced the family name. They disowned me—said as far as my family was concerned I'd been killed in action. My parents had both signed it.

'I could have handled just Dad. Our relationship had always been stormy and strained anyway. But my mom had always been my gentle ally. I had a visiting day coming up, and I'd been dying to see her. I'd been holding on for that. I guess they knew what they were doing with the padded cell, because I went berserk.

'I was at home. I was in the United States. And I was no closer to coke with ice cubes, and there'd never be a mother to run to again.

'Eventually, I learned to handle prison the same way I learned to handle 'Nam. By accepting it as my reality and forgetting everything else.

'There's not a whole lot of good that can be said about prison. Except maybe this—that your pride and dignity and worth as a human being is deep inside you, where nobody can take it away. At first, I thought they could. They did, too. But they stopped trying when they realised I was getting stronger instead of weaker. I served six months.

'The first thing I did when I got out was bought a glass of coke—with extra ice. The second was to go back to the only thing I had left to love—rodeo.'

Cory was crying softly as he finished. 'Oh, Dallas,' she finally managed to croak, 'I'm so sorry.'

His smile, as his eyes met hers, was tired and

sad. 'Don't be,' he drawled softly. 'It was a long time ago.'

She tried to remember when he'd said that to her once before. That night they'd gone to dinner, when he'd told her his parents were dead.

Her voice was trembling with emotion. 'They're not really dead, are they?'

For a moment bitterness, raw and angry, flared in his eyes. But he looked away from her, gazing steadfastly into the trees. Then his shoulders squared with resolve, and he met her eyes again, his now cold. His voice was flat. 'They were killed in action,' he stated softly, but there was no ignoring the band of steel that ran chillingly through those words.

'Dallas, that phone call—that had something to do with your parents, didn't it?'

'Yes,' he affirmed coldly, not asking how she knew about it.

A terrible suspicion dawned on her. 'They've tried before, haven't they?'

'Leave it alone, Cory,' he warned crisply.

'No! Tell me if they've tried before,' she demanded shrilly.

He shrugged as if this conversation bored him. 'Okay, Cory. My mom's been writing since about two years after I got out of prison. I return her letters unopened. Are you satisfied?'

'Satisfied?' she asked with dismay. 'How could you, Dallas? Oh, I don't deny that it's a terrible thing they did. It was cruel, and outrageous, and stupid. But don't you think by writing maybe they were prepared to admit that they reacted out of anger and humiliation, and that they were sorry?

'Damn you, Dallas! It's not them in the wrong anymore. It's you! You, with your stupid stubborn pride. Don't you think you've got them back by

now? After all these years, that the hurting has
gone on long enough? How many pounds of flesh
are you going to demand before you're satisfied?
Or maybe you're never going to be satisfied!
Maybe you're going to let them die without
ever——'

'Shut up, Cory!' His eyes blazed with angry blue
sparks.

'Dallas,' she said, not backing down, but
becoming calmer. 'Forgive them. And if you can't
do it for yourself, do it for me and our children—
their grandchildren. Please?'

'No.'

'Dallas, don't you see what this hatred has
done to you, and will keep doing? You told me
that you were a worse cripple than Missy, and you
were right. But I can't make it better. The solution
is inside you.'

He regarded her silently, his look cold and
assessing. 'Everything has changed between us,
hasn't it, Cory?' he asked softly, but his voice was
devoid of warmth.

'Of course not,' she stammered, taken aback
that he would reach that conclusion.

'Funny,' he said softly, and with terrifying
remoteness, 'funny—I feel like it has.' He turned
and walked away.

She cried again that night, lying in bed and
thinking of all that he'd told her. She ached with a
pain that was almost physical when she imagined
him in prison. Dallas, her beautiful free spirit,
caged up. He would have been like a lion behind
bars, restless, pacing, tense, and yet still proud.
And beneath those watchful eyes would have been
the fear and uncertainty and loneliness that he'd
learned never to show.

No wonder he was so cautious with his love! So

guarded, so reluctant to trust or love again. She wrestled with his parting phrase. Things hadn't changed. If it was possible she loved him even more. And yet she understood why he thought they had. Because people who he had loved with all his heart and soul had betrayed him before, and now his expectations of people, even of her, were twisted with cynicism.

Tomorrow, she told herself, he would have had time to think about it. Tomorrow she would reassure him, and tell him all over again how much she loved him. And tomorrow, she would have to try and convince him again that he had to reconcile with his parents.

But the next day, she stared at Dutch, stunned. 'What did you say?' she whispered.

'He's gone, Cory,' Dutch repeated in a voice gruff with sympathy.

'He probably just went for a drive or some——

'Cory,' Dutch interrupted gently. 'He took everything he owns.' He hesitated. 'I don't think he's coming back.'

CHAPTER TEN

IT was several days before Cory could accept the fact that he was gone, because although he had physically removed every reminder of himself, his spirit lingered in everything he had touched. If she looked long enough, and hard enough, she felt like she could still see him holding his powerful mount in check as he galloped in for dinner at night. And if she closed her eyes and listened fiercely, she was certain that she could hear his low laughter joining that of the others when they sat around the dinner table. But when she opened her eyes again, and looked eagerly and longingly at his place at the table, his chair would be empty, though the laughter would remain in her mind, haunting her heart.

And at night, lying in bed, she would quietly open the door and invite the memories in to dance and play in her mind. She would remember the first time his lips had touched hers, the feel of her hand in his, the midnight blue of his eyes as they lingered on her face. Each scene played before her, and she clung to it, for the pain of remembering was far more comforting than the pain of letting go.

She remembered, in exacting detail, how he had held Missy on the horse in front of him, how they had danced together, the long sunny afternoons they had spent working with that filly. The memories beckoned her more seductively than reality, and slowly she retired from the world, reaching a point where she no longer had any desire to get out of bed in the mornings. And one day, to her surprise, the memories didn't hurt anymore, were no longer capable of penetrating the numbness that enveloped her.

'I don't feel anything,' she marvelled dully. 'It doesn't hurt at all.'

And it didn't. Emotion seemed to have fled her, leaving a hollowed shell. She had not cried, and she vowed that she would not, not for Dallas, not for herself, not for anybody, ever again.

Tilda brought her trays and tried frantically to get her to talk or to eat. But Cory only looked at her, with eyes far too old. Mac, too came in every day, full of false cheer, and though Cory responded to him, he noticed her smile was brittle, and her eyes remote.

Finally, he grew irritated. 'Look, Cor, you got to quit feeling sorry for yourself. I know you loved him. I know that you must feel like your heart is so busted up it's never going to heal. But you're young, and it will, and there'll be others.'

'Loved him?' she echoed blankly.

'Dallas,' her father said, feeling sudden fear.

'I didn't love him,' Cory denied stonily. 'I didn't.'

'Sure, sweetheart, sure,' Mac said patting her hand with real concern.

'I think she's going crazy,' he told Tilda later. 'I think we'd better call a doctor.'

The doctor looked into Cory's wan face and sunken eyes. 'Cory, it's me, Dr Luke.'

'Hello, Dr Luke,' she said woodenly.

'I hear you're not feeling very well. You've already used up your quota of sick days for this year.'

His attempt at humour was not responded to 'I'm feeling fine,' Cory informed him, meeting his eyes unwinkingly.

'Are you trying to die?' he asked her softly.

For a moment there was a startled light in the lifeless eyes, but it died, and she gave him the faintest semblance of a smile. 'Of course not.'

He frowned. 'Cory, Mac and Tilda told me a little about you and Dallas. Maybe we should talk about that.'

She shook her head firmly.

The doctor sighed, helplessly. 'Cory, I'm going to give you a shot. It'll help you sleep.'

'I'd like that,' she said tiredly, and moments later drifted to sleep for the first time in days.

'Well?' Tilda asked the doctor anxiously when he emerged from the room.

'She's in mourning, Tilda, and there's not a lot that can be done to rush the process. She's young and strong and healthy, and she'll work it through. Meanwhile, all you can do is keep after her to eat and talk and cry. Especially to cry. I'll drop back next week. If things haven't improved we'll decide where to go from there.'

But they did improve. It was Cameron who unwittingly broke the spell. He went into her darkened room and looked at her shrunken form self-consciously. 'I brought you some pictures,' he stammered uneasily, reached into his pocket and handed her the snapshots.

There was no sign of tenderness in her face as she looked at his newborn son, nor any sign of a smile as she got to the ones he had taken the day the washer spilled over.

And then she stopped, and her eyes widened as she studied one of the pictures. Dallas stood over her, dumping suds over her head, and she was holding her arms up impotently against the onslaught and laughing. He was laughing too, the laughter making his face look incredibly handsome and vibrant. But it was the look in his eyes that made her catch her breath. They were fastened on her upturned face with an expression she hadn't noticed at the time. A strange wistfulness lurked below the laughter, something like the look of a little boy looking through the window of a pet store at a puppy he's never going to be able to have.

Slowly, she turned the picture over, and closed her eyes, feeling the tears squeeze out from behind her lashes.

'Cory, I'm sorry!' Cameron exclaimed desperately. 'I thought they'd cheer you up.'

She opened her eyes, and smiled shakily at him. 'They have, Cameron. It's okay. Everything's okay.'

Cameron tumbled out of the room, and down the steps. 'Tilda! Gosh, I'm sorry. I don't know what I did. She's crying.'

Tilda stared at his frightened face—and then enveloped him in an enthusiastic hug. 'She's crying? Praise the Lord!'

'What?' Cameron asked, as though he seriously doubted Tilda's sanity. 'I don't get it.'

'There are only two things that can heal a hurt like Cory's, Cameron. One of them isn't going to happen. The other is tears.' She gave him a radiant smile, and loped up the stairs.

Cory was still staring at the picture racked by sobs. She met Tilda's eyes and cried harder.

'I loved him,' she choked. 'Oh, God, Tilda, how I loved him! He loved me, too, Tilda. And he still went away. It hurts. It hurts so bad!'

Tilda took the sobbing girl and laid her head against her ample bosom, stroking her head tenderly. 'I know,' she crooned lovingly. 'I know.'

Cory carried on for over an hour, the pain

flushing itself out of her on waves of tears. And when she finally drew her head away from Tilda, there was strength as well as sadness in her living eyes. 'I'm a little bit hungry,' she said, and Tilda smiled at her with warmth and understanding.

It was almost a week before she had regained her strength enough to get out of bed, and on the first day, she insisted Mac saddle Wings for her. Without hesitating, she rode out to the pond, and found herself smiling with tenderness at the memories it conjured up for her.

. . . I'm looking for mermaids . . . it's one of my favourite pastimes . . . give me a break, Cory . . . there isn't a man alive who wouldn't have watched . . . and Dallas is the nicest man in the whole world . . . are you going to marry him, Cory . . .?

'I loved,' Cory told herself firmly. 'And even though it hurts, I'm so glad I loved. I could have lived my whole life without knowing what it was like.'

She knew, in a way, that it was a sentence, too. For life would never be quite the same again. No one and no one thing would ever be able to fill the gap in her that Dallas had left. Never again would her heart sing a song as vibrant and soaring as the one it had sung for him.

But there would always be the memories. Nothing could take those from her, and knowing what it was to love made the tremendous price of pain worth paying.

She turned Wings away from the pond. Life would be less intense without him, and she would have to live without the pinnacles, but live it she would! She touched her feet to Wings' sides and allowed herself to appreciate the gentle pleasure of the wind on her cheeks.

Time marched on, and life moved on. Timmy

called once. He said only that he had heard she wasn't well, and hoped she was feeling better.

'I am, Timmy. I'm much better.'

He hesitated. 'There's a dance this weekend if you wanted to——' His voice trailed away.

'No. Thanks anyway.'

'It was different with you and him, wasn't it Cory? Like the real thing.'

She laughed softly. 'Yes, just like the real thing, Timmy. Complete with fireworks.'

'Send me a postcard from Europe, okay?' He sounded defeated.

'I will,' she said gently, and replaced the receiver on its hook.

Shorty was no longer on the ranch, though Cory could never quite bring herself to ask whether he'd left on his own, or been fired. Sometimes she wondered if anything would have been different if she had just let the wind take that letter out of her hand that day. Or if she'd told Dallas about it. Maybe then they could have worked things through more slowly. But she knew better than to torture herself with maybes.

Shelly came over one day to display her and Cameron's treasure—Travis Jesse. Again the maybe haunted her—if she hadn't have heard that heartbroken voice that day she had tried to call Shelly, would she have been so insistent that he make peace?

She forced herself away from the thought. 'What a good name,' she said to Shelly, 'for a little boy destined to grow into a cowboy.'

Shelly pressed the baby into her arms, and looking into his tiny, wrinkled face, and feeling his small fist close around her finger, she had felt the first surge of pure and ecstatic joy since Dallas had gone. His wrinkled features held a bold and beautiful reminder for her that life would still hold moments of delight.

And then the time came to start packing the contents of the house. It was a terrible chore, but Cory attacked it with vigour. As much as she loved this place, it was haunted now by the love that had blossomed here, and now lay in ashes. She knew as long as she remained on the Flying M she would never be able to forget, and she knew it was time now to start forgetting.

Mac was busy buying tickets, and talking to travel agents, and she smiled at his enthusiasm, and allowed herself to be drawn into the circle of his and Tilda's excitement.

Together they would sit around the kitchen table, surrounded by boxes, and plot their course across Europe. Mac planned each step of the journey, complete to where he wanted to eat, and what he wanted to see. His new bible was a tattered and obviously out-dated volume of a book called *Europe on Five Dollars a Day*, that he had purchased for a dime at a used book store.

'There's a real live prince at this castle,' he said showing Cory the picture of the castle, 'so don't you go wearing that foamy dress.'

Cory smiled, remembering how once that dress had made her feel like Cinderella. 'I think we're only allowed one prince per lifetime, Dad.' And for a moment a sad and awkward silence hung over them.

The last week was a whirl of activity that seemed to make the parting easier. The house was cleaned to sparkling, and personal possessions were finding their way into suitcases.

There were so many goodbyes to be said, and Cory saved the last one for Missy. She knocked firmly at the door of the modest little house and Mrs Henderson let her in.

Missy greeted her coolly, betrayal written in her eyes.

'I came to say goodbye,' Cory said, faltering.

'Everybody I like always leaves,' Missy stated angrily. 'My daddy, and Dallas, and you.'

'Missy—I'm sorry.'

'He used to come here, you know. He used to come here almost every night and play checkers with me.' Cory remembered assuming that he had spent all those evenings with Nancy.

'You could have married him,' Missy continued shrilly, 'I know you could have, because he loved you. And then you both could have stayed here, and sometimes we could have gone riding together.'

Cory crouched down beside her, and took one of her cold little hands in hers. 'I loved him too, Missy.'

The little girl's eyes fastened wide and startled on Cory's face, and Cory felt the tears beginning to run down her cheeks.

'Did you?' Missy asked, touching Cory's cheek with a small finger. 'Then why did he go?'

'I don't know for sure, Missy. But you know how you feel right now? Like you're so hurt and torn up inside that you're afraid ever to love anybody again? I think that's how Dallas felt for a long time, before he even met us. I think maybe he was afraid of loving us. Afraid that it would hurt too much.'

'Dallas wasn't scared of anything!'

'Except that, Missy,' Cory corrected her softly.

'We would have never hurt him, Cory.'

'Sometimes, when people love each other, they hurt each other without meaning to.'

'Is he coming back, Cory?' Missy whispered.

Cory bit her lip. Hearing the question, she knew

that she, too, had hoped, somewhere in the far reaches of her mind, that he would come back. And now she knew, for both of them, that she had to lay that hope to rest once and for all. 'He's not coming back, Missy,' she said firmly. 'He's never coming back.'

Missy opened her arms, and Cory hugged her, feeling her warm tears splashing down her neck.

Missy released her hold on Cory and stared at her hands. 'Will you come back, Cory? Will you come back, and see me, and maybe take me riding?'

'You know I will, love. And I'll send you postcards, too. How does that sound?

Missy nodded.

'Goodbye, Missy.'

''Bye, Cory. Have a wonderful trip,' the little girl said bravely.

'I'm going to try, sweetie,' Cory returned just as bravely, and then quickly turned on her heel and left before the tears could start again.

It was late that night when she pulled on an old sweater and went into the yard, touching with gentle eyes all that had been her life, and wishing it a heartfelt farewell.

Slowly, she walked into the embrace of the night and strolled across a field to the little grove where her mother was buried. It looked beautiful in the moonlight, and she sank down beside the headstone, brushing her hands tenderly across the words etched in granite.

'Hi, Mom,' she whispered slowly. 'I'll bet you know we're leaving tomorrow. I'll come back with flowers sometimes, if it's all right with the new owner.' Her eyes trailed around the little grove, and she continued in a whisper.

'Do you think I'll ever love again, Mom? Ever

feel again what I felt when his arms were around me? Ever feel my heart begin to pound within my chest just because of the colour of the eyes that are resting on my face?'

She was crying softly, now, knowing why she had come to this place. Knowing it was finally to say the goodbye that hurt the worst. It was here that she had buried love once before, and now she would lie down the other to sleep peacefully beside it.

'Goodbye, Dallas,' she wept softly. 'Wherever you are, my love, I pray that you find the peace and the happiness I couldn't give you.'

The hands that rested suddenly and gently on her shoulders neither startled her or broke into her grief.

'Oh, Daddy,' she finally whispered brokenly, squeezing her eyes shut against the waves and waves of slow hurt that washed over her. There was no answer, and her eyes flew open again. She turned her head slowly. The man who stood behind her, his legs apart, and his hands resting on her shoulders, was not Mac. He looked like a mountain carved out of the evening sky, and her heart began to pound joyously in recognition.

'Dallas?' she asked incredulously, struggling shakily to her feet. 'Dallas,' she whispered touching his face. And then she cried, 'Dallas!' and fell sobbing against his chest. He said nothing, and his arms did not fold around her.

'Dallas,' she took a step back from him and gazed at his face sombrely. It was a study in anguish. 'I love you,' she whispered, the tears gathering in her eyes, and then with a tormented groan he reached for her and gathered her into his arms.

'How could you?' he murmured against her hair.

'After what I've done to you, how can you still love me?'

'Love doesn't just go away, Dallas. Not even if you want it to, and not even if you say it has.'

'I'm finally beginning to understand that,' he murmured, and his lips eagerly sought hers, and claimed them to be his own.

'Marry me, Cory,' he whispered into her ear. 'Please.'

'Mr Dallas Hawthorne,' she smiled, 'you've got yourself a deal.' Suddenly, she backed away from him, placing her hands on her small hips, and scowling, though her eyes shone. 'Where have you been? Why didn't you tell me where you were going? This had better not be your pattern for dealing with conflict, Mr Hawthorne!'

He smiled down at her. 'Don't you sound married?' he teased, and she blushed, but he became instantly serious. 'I went home, Cory. When I left here, that isn't where I intended to go. I'd convinced myself that you couldn't accept me the way I was, and that I wasn't going to change. But I think if I'm really honest, that wasn't the whole reason. I think, perversely, I wanted to hurt you the way I'd been hurt. See if you'd be quite so eager to preach forgiveness if you'd been the one walked away from. It was crazy and it was cruel,' he ran a tender finger down her cheek, 'and yet you're still standing here, forgiving me.

'My temper started to cool after about four hundred miles of lonely road, and I started to think about some of the things you'd said. Especially about what hate was doing to me, and I knew, then, that I could never love you the way you deserved to be loved with the hate living and growing inside me like a cancer. And I thought about what you'd said about leaving things too late, and began to worry that maybe I already had.

'You see, the phone call that morning was from my mother. My dad was dying and she begged me to come home and make peace.

'As soon as I saw him, I knew I didn't hate him anymore. I guess I knew I probably never had. We had two weeks. I couldn't get over how easy he was to talk to, or how much we had to say to each other.

'It was really close to the end when he asked about prison. I would have rather not told him, because I knew it was going to hurt him more than it ever hurt me. But it seemed really important to him, so I told him, trying to gloss over the worst of it.

'He was crying when I was done. I'd never in my whole life seen my father cry. "Dallas," he said finally, "I know you've forgiven me, and I'm going to my grave content in the knowledge my son's become a bigger and better man than I ever was. You see, I can't ever forgive you. You fought me every turn of the way for your whole life. Why didn't you come back and fight me on that one? I don't think a day went by in all those years when I didn't imagine you showing up on my doorstep, fighting mad and ready to take me on. All those lost years . . ." I thought he was going to start crying again—hell, I was—but he didn't. He smiled.

'"Ever tell you I met Mel Rasmusen at a country club dance?" he asked me with this huge grin. "I knocked the snivelling little jerk's teeth out. I loved you, son. I love you." And then he died, still smiling.

'We were a lot alike, the old man and I. We both seem to have inherited more pride and stubbornness than what's good for a man. Probably,' he teased, 'more than what's good for the women who marry us, too.'

She sensed, joyfully, that all the pieces of the puzzle were in place. Dallas was whole, and he was hers. The past had no claim on him. She entered his arms, and his mouth met hers with drive and power and passion. He kissed her as a man kisses a woman—the woman he loves.

The next morning Cory bounded into the kitchen feeling as though her soul had sprouted wings. 'Where's Dallas?' she demanded of Tilda.

'In the meeting,' Tilda replied, putting away the last of the dishes, and looking at her watch. 'I have to go, too.'

Cory glared at her. 'What meeting? And how come everyone's been invited, except me?'

Tilda shrugged. 'I guess you're not an employee of the ranch, Cory. You just live here. Maybe you could make sure all your things are ready to go.'

'Thanks a bunch,' Cory muttered, but went up to her room to do a last minute check, anyway. It didn't even look like her room, she thought. Without the beautiful patchwork quilt, and her big four poster bed the room lacked personality, and in fact looked drab, and much in need of a paint job.

She sighed, and sank down on the dismantled mattress. She was going to be Dallas' wife. Home wasn't a bedroom, or a house, or a ranch. Not anymore. Home was where he was.

'Well,' Mac said, delighting as always in any occasion that could be handled with even a pretence of businesslike decorum, 'I guess you're all wondering why I called you to this here meeting. Truth to tell is that I wanted personally to turn over the reins to the new owner of the Flying M.

'Who isn't here yet,' Dutch reminded him gruffly.

Cameron shifted positions with unveiled boredom, and Dutch looked at his boots, not even pretending interest in what Mac had to say.

Mac ignored them and continued, clearing his throat. 'I think I told you all how impressed I was when I first met the new owner of the Flying M. I think I said then that he was young and ambitious and could turn the Flying M around. I've met with this man several times since then, and my first impression still holds. He's a good man, who knows ranching, and likes to get his hands dirty. He ain't the kind who'll be mailing you orders from Timbuctoo.

'I personally guarantee that none of you could ask for a better man to work for—'ceptin maybe me, of course—and I want to ask each of you to give him the kind of loyalty you've always given me.' He paused, and took a deep breath, obviously winding up to continue his long-winded recital, when Dutch cut him off impatiently.

'I like to make my own decisions about a man, Mac.'

Cameron nodded his agreement and Mac scowled at them both.

'Fine,' he snapped. 'I won't say anymore. But I want you both to know that you've destroyed one of my finest moments. It's not everyday that a man gets to make a speech, you know.' He looked sulky. 'I practised and everything.'

Dutch was unsympathetic. 'At least you could tell us his name before he gets here.'

The twinkle reappeared instantly in Mac's eyes.

'He already is here, gentlemen. His name,' he paused for effect, 'is Mr Dallas Hawthorne.'

A stunned silence hung over the tiny room. Dallas shook his head to the chair Mac was ceremoniously holding out for him behind the desk, moving instead beside it, and hitching one long leg over a corner. Everyone began talking at once. Dallas waited patiently for the noise to stop, but when it continued unabated he rose.

'It's been my experience,' he broke in quietly, commanding immediate silence, 'that when a ranch changes hands it causes a lot of tension and stress for the people who work there. The unfortunate result is that the ranch runs either better or worse than it usually would, and it can take months to build the kind of trust it takes for things to return to normal so that you can see what you've really got.

'I've seen what I've really got. The Flying M is a good ranch, staffed by knowledgeable people and hard workers. I'm proud of it and I'm proud of you.

'I'd like to announce a few changes to the structure of the personnel on the ranch. Cameron, Mac tells me that you've been acting foreman, and that you've done a fine job. You're as level-headed and as good a cowboy as any I've ever worked with, and I'm hoping you'll accept the position permanently.'

Cameron's jaw dropped, and his eyes began to shine as he digested what Dallas had told him. 'I can't believe it—of course I will.'

'Good. I've heard some rumours that Shelly is one fine cook, and since we're losing the best cook in the area, I'd like to ask her to join our team. The deal would include this house, if she accepts. I'm going to build a new one for my wife.'

Cameron scrambled out of his chair. 'I've got to

call Shelly.' He stopped before he reached the door, and turned slowly back to Dallas. 'Your wife?'

Dallas turned to Mac. 'If I still have your permission?'

Mac ran a wrinkled sleeve over his eyes. 'I just want her to be happy, Dallas. It was all I could do not to tell her you'd be back someday, when she was so sick.'

'I haven't told her about this yet. I'd appreciate a few minutes alone with her.'

'Sure,' Mac agreed readily. 'I was just going to pour everyone a toast in the living room. Cor,' he shouted up the stairs after everyone had left the den. 'Come and meet the new owner.'

She scampered down the steps, and her eyes flew around the gathering in the living room. Dallas wasn't among them, and she wondered if that meant the new owner hadn't given him a job.

'He's in the office,' Mac said flicking a thumb at the door. 'Just go in. He's waiting for you.'

'Waiting for me?' Cory asked, baffled. 'Why?'

Mac shrugged, and squaring her shoulders she opened the office door.

Dallas was leaning casually against the desk, his arms folded across his chest, and his eyes resting on her.

She glanced around. 'Dad told me the new owner wanted to see me, and that he was in here.'

Dallas said nothing, and suddenly her eyes flew back to him, widening at his wink.

'You?' she whispered, being afraid to believe it, but at his nod she flew across the room into his arms. 'Really, Dallas?' She looked at him with slightly awed and shining eyes.

'Really,' he affirmed softly, stroking her hair gently.

'But how? I thought you were just a cowboy!'

He laughed softly. 'I am just a cowboy, Cory. I did fairly well in rodeo for a number of years, but it finally dawned on me that I was never going to be the best. It was strictly a physical handicap. I'm about six inches taller than a really good rodeo cowboy can be.

'Anyway, I knew that being young and determined and enthusiastic was only going to keep me in the money for so long. At the same time I had a friend who had a handicap more severe than mine. He'd lost both his legs, but that wasn't the real handicap. The real handicap was that nobody would give him a chance to prove he still had a brilliant mind. And with my record, I knew nobody was going to line up to give me a chance once I was washed up at rodeo either. We'd been branded losers, but we were also rebels enough not to accept the label. We formed a partnership.

'I won the money, and he invested it. He was sharp and shrewd and a gambler, and his pay-offs were big. I've bought a few ranches over the years because of his investments, but it wasn't until I saw this one that I knew I'd finally found the place that I could settle down.' He paused and added softly, 'I wonder if it had anything to do with the little boy saddling a horse in the yard the first morning I drove in?'

She pulled away from him and looked at him reproachfully. 'Why didn't you tell me before, Dallas?'

'Cory, I was more tempted than I've ever been in my life. That night when we had dinner, and you told me what your dream was, I wanted right then and there to give it to you. But you didn't know everything, then, and I wasn't sure that you'd be able to accept what I had to tell you. Knowing how much you loved this place made me wonder if you'd marry me for that—or for me.

'I had to know it was for me and me alone.'

Her eyes were brilliant and shining with love as she accepted the invitation of his open arms. Their lips joined in an ecstatic celebration of their love. He ran tender lips over the soft curve of her neck. And when he looked at her again, his eyes held a spark of desire.

'I told my mother to be here next Saturday for a wedding. I hope that isn't too soon. It seems like I've spent my whole life waiting for you to happen to me, Cory. I can't wait anymore.'

'I'll have to see if Missy's free,' she murmured contentedly into his chest. 'I want her to be our flower girl. And I'll have to see if Madame Marcelle can get a dress ready that fast—but if she can't will you accept me in blue jeans?'

'I fell in love with a lady who wears blue jeans. I can sure as hell marry her looking the same way.'

There was no need to announce what had passed between them when they finally emerged from behind the closed office door. It glowed softly and proudly in both their faces.

Dallas gazed into her eyes, and then held up a hand for silence. 'Cory and I are getting married on Saturday. We'd be honoured if you could all attend.'

The bedlam caused by that announcement had hardly died away when Mac cleared his throat gruffly.

'I got an announcement to make, too. I hate to steal you guys' thunder,' he managed to sound quite contrite, despite the gleeful glimmer in his eyes, 'but Tilda and I are going to tie the knot, too.'

'Dad! Tilda!' Cory hugged them both enthusiastic-ally.

'Thank God you and your cowboy are on again,' Mac said gruffly. 'Tilda and I are planning on getting married in London, and I don't think, much as we both love you Cory, that either of us was looking forward to having you on the honeymoon.'

'Mac!' Tilda reproached him.

'Oh, hell!' Mac exclaimed suddenly. 'I've got to cancel some tickets or miss my little girl's wedding.' He started to dash for the phone, and then stopped, his eyes fastened on the window.

'Well, I'll be darned! It's starting to snow.'

Dallas' eyes sought Cory's and she nodded. He came to her, and smiling they went out into the soft, gentle swirling snowflakes.

'I like things that are unpredictable,' he said, his eyes running over her face with tender apprecia-tion.

'I'm starting to,' she responded, her dancing eyes on his.

'Let's go to the pond,' he suggested softly.

'The pond? Dallas, it's hardly the time for a swim.'

His grin was boyish and loving. 'But it's just the right time to pick a building site for our house.'

'Our house,' she echoed dreamily. 'Oh, Dallas, do you think there will ever be a house again that will hold as much love and laughter as ours will?'

His lips met hers in answer, and it seemed suddenly as though she had reached one of those magnificent, snow-capped peaks in the distance. Her heart soared on fluttering wings through the brilliant sky of his eyes and she knew she was where she truly belonged—forever.

The ice cold snow went down her back, and she

shrieked with delighted rage as he dashed away from her, and across the snow to the path that would lead them to the pond. She took chase, noting with an inward smile that he slowed his long strides so that she could catch him.

He reached back, offering a hand to her, and she took it, running abreast with him. They ran hand in hand through the huge wet snowflakes, and their pealing laughter ran across the muted snow with the sparkling promise of summer ever after.

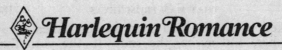

Coming Next Month

2773 SHADOWS OF EDEN Rosemary Badger
Meeting a handsome wealthy author is just what the
survivor of an accident that claimed her family needed—
until her feelings turn to love and he starts to pull away.

2774 SAND CASTLES Meg Dominique
The manager of Florida's Hotel Fandango is ready to settle
down, while his ladylove doesn't dare stay in one place
long enough to get involved. Yet when he holds her in his
arms anything seems possible.

2775 AGE OF CONSENT Victoria Gordon
Despite the crush she once had on him, an out-of-work
journalist turns to a writer in Tasmania for help—only to
find that he and his beautiful girlfriend add to her worries.

2776 POWER POINT Rowan Kirby
A child psychologist puts her heart at risk when she breaks
all her rules of professional detachment in order to help a
dynamic documentary producer reach his young brother.

2777 BLUEBELLS ON THE HILL Barbara McMahon
In the peaceful Sierra Nevada, a rancher, still bitter over the
desertion of his wife, opens up to a woman who can't tell
him she isn't exactly what she seems.

2778 RETURN TO FARAWAY Valerie Parv
A film producer returns to the Australian Outback at her
estranged husband's invitation. Or so she thinks. But his
resentful teenage daughter from a previous marriage is up
to her old tricks!

Available in July wherever paperback books are sold, or
through Harlequin Reader Service.

In the U.S.
901 Fuhrmann Blvd.
P.O. Box 1397
Buffalo, N.Y. 14240-1397

In Canada
P.O. Box 2800, Postal Station A
5170 Yonge Street
Willowdale, Ontario M2N 6J3

Harlequin "Super Celebration" SWEEPSTAKES

NEW PRIZES—NEW PRIZE FEATURES & CHOICES—MONTHLY

---

1. To enter the sweepstakes, follow the instructions outlined on the Center Insert Card. Alternate means of entry, NO PURCHASE NECESSARY, you may also enter by mailing your name, address and birthday on a plain 3" x 5" piece of paper to: In U.S.A.: Harlequin "Super Celebration" Sweepstakes, P.O. Box 1867, Buffalo, N.Y. 14240-1867. In Canada: Harlequin "Super Celebration" Sweepstakes, P.O. Box 2800, 5170 Yonge Street, Postal Station A, Willowdale, Ontario M2N 6J3.

2. Winners will be selected in random drawings from all entries received. All prizes will be awarded. These prizes are in addition to any free gifts which might be offered. Versions of this sweepstakes with different prizes may appear in other presentations by TorStar and their affiliates. The maximum value of the prizes offered is $8,000.00. Winners selected will receive the prize offered from their prize package.

3. The selection of winners will be conducted under the supervision of Marden-Kane, an independent judging organization. By entering the sweepstakes, each entrant accepts and agrees to be bound by these rules and the decision of the judges which shall be final and binding. Odds of winning are dependent upon the total number of entries received. Taxes, if any, are the sole responsibility of the winners. Prizes are not transferable. This sweepstakes is scheduled to appear in Retail Outlets of Harlequin Books during the period of June 1986 to December 1986. All entries must be received by January 31st, 1987. The drawing will take place on or about March 1st, 1987 at the offices of Marden-Kane, Lake Success, New York. For Quebec (Canada) residents, any litigation regarding the running of this sweepstakes and the awarding of prizes must be submitted to La Regie de Lotteries et Course du Quebec.

4. This presentation offers the prizes as illustrated on the Center Insert Card.

5. This offer is open to residents of the U.S., and Canada, 18 years or older, except employees of TorStar, its affilliates, subsidiaries, Marden-Kane and all other agencies and persons connected with conducting this sweepstakes. All Federal, State and local laws apply. Void where prohibited or restricted by law. Winners will be notified by mail and may be required to execute an affidavit of eligibility and release which must be returned within 14 days after notification. Winners consent to the use of their name, photograph and/or likeness for advertising and publicity in conjunction with this and similar promotions without additional compensation. One prize per family or household. Canadian winners will be required to answer a skill testing question.

6. For a list of our most recent prize winners, send a stamped, self-addressed envelope to: WINNERS LIST, c/o Marden-Kane, P.O. Box 525, Sayreville, NJ 08872.

No Lucky Number needed to win!

Janet
Dailey
Americana

A romantic tour of America with Janet Dailey!

Enjoy the first two releases of this collection of your favorite previously published Janet Dailey titles, presented alphabetically state by state.

Alabama ~ Alaska